Zero Gravity
by Tom LaMarr

Printed in the United States of America.
Published by Marcinson Press, Jacksonville, Florida
© Copyright 2017 by Tom LaMarr

ISBN 978-1-946932-02-0

Published by
Marcinson Press
10950-60 San Jose Blvd., Suite 136
Jacksonville, FL 32223 USA
http://www.marcinsonpress.com

Find Zero Gravity on Facebook:
www.facebook.com/zerogravitybook/

Find Tom LaMarr on the web:
www.tomlamarr.com

ZERO
GRAVITY

FOR ALLIE

CHAPTER ONE

Game Changer

A runner waited on third, Tampa trailed by two points, and a red-haired Minor League player who went by the name Hank Fielding stood ready to become the most famous batter ever. From Canadian Mounties to monks in Tibet, people all over the world would be talking about the incredible feat I witnessed firsthand.

It's strange enough that I was there. A chunky kid who bagged at sports, I had never paid much attention to baseball or football or any of the other games Dad watched on TV. Yet there I sat, close to third, looking out across the visitors' dugout. Dad leaned forward from the seat to my left.

Though he was too smart to ever say it, I knew Dad had always been disappointed that none of my interests involved hitting or kicking a ball. A baseball player himself way back in college, he wanted a son he could cheer from the stands, or at least sit with at games. And when he told me the Sunday before how he got "these incredible tickets," he was looking at me with wide, imploring eyes like a dog begging for pizza crusts. "It'll be great. The Brevard County Manatees versus our own Tampa Yankees." Then he said something to seal the deal. Molly and Mom would stay home. "It's just you and me, Adam." This, I knew, would make Molly jealous, which suddenly made it worthwhile.

Game day came. April 22nd. I remember because I had a full day of school before the evening game and it was Earth Day. Ms.

Voll, our civics teacher who would have been a hippie if she'd been born a lot earlier, made it her lesson for all of fifth period. She told us about Gaia, the ancient belief that Earth was a living being. "Mother Earth can live without us," she said, pushing back a strand of wavy red hair. "But we can't live without her."

I liked Ms. Voll because she always came up with super smart sayings. Like the one she ended her class with that day: "The world will end with a whimper, not a bang."

But as smart as she was, I don't think she knew it would start that evening.

When Dad and I took our seats in the stadium, I was happy to see I was far from the heaviest one there. All around me, big adults squeezed into their spaces. Like hanging out at the mall, I felt almost average, and average felt good. As the sun slowly made its way down behind us, a breeze that smelled like bratwurst and popcorn kept the humidity in check. This was good for a kid who didn't like being all sweaty, an easy enough thing to be in Florida. Dad got us a snack. The nachos tasted great. "They better," he laughed, "at two dollars a chip."

The only thing that seemed unnecessary was the game itself. With all the waiting and standing around, baseball moved liked a video game that was constantly freezing up to re-buffer. The biggest surprise came in the sixth inning when the nighttime lights went supernova, making the Astroturf an even faker green and painting the sky orange-gray.

This was not how Dad viewed the game. Right from the opening pitch, he looked like he was in heaven, or as close as he could get without having an actual bat in his grip, waiting for the pitcher to deliver the perfect fastball. I didn't get to see him like this too often. Though he couldn't have been a bigger optimist – "Sales at the store are going to pick up" – he always looked a little sad. Watching him that night, smiling, cheering, dripping cheese on his shirt, I felt glad to be with him.

And when Hank Fielding, the Tampa batter who was about to become super famous, leaned into the plate, I had to admit I was paying attention.

"C'mon," Dad said quietly, "eyes on the ball."

The pitcher's arm moved in a blur. The batter connected with a stinging *khhk*! The bright white ball lifted into the air. It didn't curve, just kept going up. The crowd gasped as one, and even I could tell the ball was rising higher than it should have been. "Mother of mothers!" shouted the man to my right. "It's out of the park. Way out of the park!"

Dad jumped up from his seat. I must have too; I was on my feet.

"Adam! Are you seeing this?"

The white speck climbed into the sky – steadily, slowly.

"There!" I heard myself shout. "You can barely see it!"

The fuzzy dot held to its course, until it faded into that orange-gray haze.

The gasps turned to cheers, a jet plane roar. Tampa fans poured onto the field, bringing the game to a halt. Dad started to speak, but didn't. He seemed too excited.

"Steroids," a woman behind us lamented. "They're ruining the game."

"Was that some kind of trick?" I asked.

"Don't know," said Dad. "But whatever it was, it was pretty amazing."

"I know one thing," I said. "I'd watch more baseball if it was all like that."

At school the next day, that ball got loads of attention, as did the kid who'd seen it firsthand and not on some grainy YouTube video.

"Adam Weaver." Our Principal stopped me in the hall between classes, which hardly seemed like a good thing. "Did I hear correctly you were at the game last night? You saw that hit?" He smiled in a way less scary than usual. "Cool."

People were saying it just kept going. Up and up and out of this world.

Six days later, it happened again, this time in Minnesota.

CHAPTER TWO

The Call to Maintain

We didn't see many mosquitoes that May. Or butterflies. Or birds. Taking flight now came with risks. Gravity was losing strength.

Two weeks into that very strange month, a woman on a motorcycle fitted with jet engines shot up a ramp to leap across the Niagara River a mile below the falls. Like the two baseballs, Double Dare Darla kept on going.

More reports followed of people floating away, most with far less effort than the jet powered Darla. A window washer in Brazil. Pole vaulters in New Zealand. A girl who didn't fasten her seat belt on a Ferris wheel in Tel Aviv. Scientists came on TV to warn us about "pockets of Zero Gravity." These outbreaks sometimes touched the ground and sometimes hovered above it. They popped up at random, disappeared just as quickly, and moved about invisibly. Stumbling into one was like walking into quicksand in a bad action movie, except you went up instead of down.

You didn't even need one of these pockets to lift off. The Low G we had everywhere would do if you came up with a way to launch yourself. And this didn't take much. I could stand in our backyard, hurl the vegetables I'd forgotten to eat with dinner into the air, and watch them drift away.

On most every point, the scientists seemed just as confused as the rest of us. For all the predictions they now made about the Drop Down – their name for gravity losing its grip – they sure hadn't seen it coming. They never could say why gravity had stopped working or for that matter how it had worked in the first place. "We always knew we'd run out of fuel and water and clean air," one geologist conceded. "But gravity... talk about being surprised."

The closest thing to an explanation came from my English teacher, Ms. Hardman (may she rest in space). She said the Earth had grown tired of lugging us around and putting up with our bad habits. As if it were saying, "I've had it with you parasites. Go find another planet to mess up."

On May 22nd, Dad came home shaken. Someone had taken off right outside the mall where he had his Radio Shack. We interrupted dinner to watch the news story. "We've all heard of carjackings and skyjackings." The Channel 4 anchor seemed much too cheerful. She smiled as she continued, "There was a new kind of jacking today at Carrolwood Mall and it ended badly for a high-school senior turned thief."

Egged on by two friends – "We only meant it as a prank" – the kid had "borrowed" a security guard's Segway, one of those two-wheeled vehicles that made mall security guards look even less like real cops. "Dude must have been guarding something else," said one of the friends. "It was just sitting there by the smoked nuts kiosk."

Channel 4 showed a video taken with a phone. It started with the skinny, long-haired prankster leaving the mall and going down a handicap ramp into the lot. Though he couldn't have been moving ten miles an hour, his hair puffed out on all sides like smoke from an Old West locomotive. "Way to go, Jake!" the phone's owner shouted. "You did it!"

A second Segway purred out of the mall, this one commandeered by a security guard built more like me. Soon, culprit and pursuer were moving across the blacktop like a mismatched pair of Roman charioteers. Jake held onto a healthy lead but must not have seen the apple-red Corvette backing out of its space. Ramming the car's rear fender, the Segway stamped a wide, crackly crater in the fiberglass exterior while catapulting its rider upward and outward.

"No," Molly shrieked, grabbing Mom's arm.

The kid tumbled as he rose, his hair sticking out like porcupine quills. "Dude," his friend added commentary, "this really sucks."

I recognized the witness they interviewed next. A woman who worked at Cajun Express in the Food Court, she wore her red uniform and talked super fast like she'd been living on energy drinks. "He just kept going higher and higher like a balloon that got away except for the fact balloons don't scream."

Dad stepped in to finish the story. "I was outside by then along with half the mall."

He picked up the remote, turned off the TV. "It was impossible to watch and harder to ignore. It seemed unreal and much too real."

The following evening, the president issued his Call to Maintain. We watched from our living room, Mom and Dad on the couch, Molly and me sprawled flat on the cool hardwood floor. "As we have all learned from our crash course in physics," he began in his most watched ever address, "gravity is one of the four fundamental forces of nature. It cannot simply disappear. Our best scientists are confident the Drop Down will level off. But until that occurs, we must take precautions." The camera zoomed in on his face. His small dark eyes looked tired and dull. His hair seemed grayer than in pictures I'd seen. "We must keep ourselves grounded – in a very literal sense. Each of us must eat more to hold his or her weight constant. We must *Maintain*."

President Lodeswirth blinked his eyes quickly three or four times. "Some will contend we can take other measures. Like the peoples of Africa and South America, we can dig and live in tunnels. Like the French and Chinese, we can sew weights into our clothing. But we are not a nation of mole people. We are not a society of jacket stuffers. We are Americans, and if we are going to survive this great challenge, we must employ a uniquely American solution."

He paused to let us weigh his words.

"By Maintaining, we can live our lives as normally as possible. We can do more than merely survive. We can prosper in a world with less gravity."

"I thought he said this was temporary," Molly protested. "I thought he said gravity would get back its strength."

Mom got up and walked toward the kitchen. "Our president..." She stopped at the door, turning back to face us. "I think he knows more than he's saying. Wouldn't you love to have a minute alone with him? Just to look him in the eyes and ask."

"He's got a tough job," said Dad. "And gravity isn't making it any easier."

The president ignored my parents. "I am making this Call to Maintain after hearing the same reports that have come your way of thin people falling up through the sky and into space. It is time we, as Americans, stop sweating our so-called obesity crisis, and look at it for what it truly is... an obesity advantage."

"Well," Dad said calmly, "survival of the fattest."

To no one's surprise, Dad already had a plan: he would go to U-Haul first thing tomorrow, hours before they opened. He would rent their biggest truck and drive it straight to Costco. He'd fill the truck with packaged food that didn't need refrigerating, bring it home, then repeat the process till Costco ran out – or we ran out of space. The Weavers would stock up on food before everyone else got the idea.

Walking across the courtyard at school the next morning, I heard a voice too familiar to me. "Bet you're happy about this." My least favorite bully, Quinton Ferrari, was somewhere behind me. "Bet you think you're smart. Like you were ahead of your time."

Unfortunately, the president's Call to Maintain had not left me feeling smart, only more self-conscious, something I wouldn't have thought possible the day before. Being overweight at Alan Shepard Middle School had never given me any kind of advantage. It had only made me a target that no one could miss. Like right at that moment with Q coming up from behind in the outdoor courtyard. I cringed, waiting to hear our school's star quarterback lob his standard "Adam, Adam, four by eight. He'll be our fif-ty-first state!"

Quinton Ferrari had always seemed small as football players went. But a "great arm" made up for a shortfall in both weight and height. It also translated to "winning season," or so I'd been told repeatedly during the Victory Assembly a few months before. It also got Q a girlfriend who deserved way better, like maybe a guy who didn't bully others – or at least came up with smarter insults.

"Is the president going to make us all be fat like you?" With no other sounds in the courtyard, apart from our footsteps, his words picked up reverb from windows and walls. No one else talked, and there were plenty of kids outside.

I kept walking, and kept my head down.

"I'm talking to you, Mr. Adam-Adam-Four-By-Eight!"

"I'm hardly four by eight," I muttered, which was true. I wasn't that big. Not then, anyway.

I felt fingers poking the back of my shoulder: the "great arm" at work.

I tried to ignore this, along with all the stares from kids who didn't bully me but liked watching. Sitting on their concrete benches, only a few looked away. The rest smirked and smiled. I kept walking.

Q poked me again in the shoulder. I moved faster. He got me again, which took the count up to one time too many. I didn't like being poked. I wasn't some cow at a fair.

Turning to face him, intending to say, "Could you please just stop," I realized Q had been jabbing me with his phone – the phone I'd just bumped from his hand. There it was, rising into the air… six feet… seven…

"Idiot," he shouted. But he should have saved that label for himself, the way he'd jumped after it.

Now, both he and the phone were slowly rising, out and away from me. His right arm stretched out as if to throw a pass and almost touched the phone. My eyes followed his bright red sports jersey, Tampa Bay Bucs, Number 13, as he continued upward.

Three other jocks stood watching; they must have been walking with him. None of them moved.

"Help me!" Q flailed his arms and legs, like he was trying to swim through the air. "Somebody, quick!"

Other kids raced over to get a better look. Others slipped into the building, probably afraid they would also lift off. Two freshman girls got shoved and knocked down.

"Do something!" Q shouted.

Dozens of thoughts rushed through my head like debris knocked loose by a sudden downpour. "What's this?" Mick Connelly asked when I handed him my backpack.

"Pass it," I said. "Knock him toward the tree."

Q's teammate thought for a second, then finally stopped looking at me like I was the dumb one. He pulled back his arm and launched the backpack. Instantly, it collided with Q, landing right between his shoulder blades. He shifted direction, heading for the tall twisting oak. I heard gasps from all around the courtyard. Q still seemed to be coming up short, missing the tree by inches.

My backpack rose straight up following the cell phone.

I heard more gasps. Q managed to snag his sock on a jagged tip that had once been a branch. He twisted around, and took hold of the limb with his hands.

I skipped Mr. White's earth science class to watch the fire crew rescue Q like they used to do with cats. Five men anchored the ladder while three more peeled Q from the limb. It took them five minutes; Q stuck to the tree like gum to a floor. Even with the tears on his face – and the wide wet spot on his jeans – kids cheered and clapped when he finally touched the ground. "Back to your classes!" ordered Principal Frick. "Everyone, now!" When Q walked past me, he looked at me like he wanted to say, "Thanks," then looked at his friends and kept quiet.

I started off in the other direction.

"You're lucky I'm in a good mood," Q finally spoke, calling after me. "That happened to be one very nice phone."

His voice sounded shaky.

Mine did not. "You're hopeless," I heard it bounce off the walls, "devoid of hope. I should have let you float away."

CHAPTER THREE

Making Waves

The moon was getting smaller. We checked on it each night before going to bed.

The weekend after school let out, I helped Dad shutter his Radio Shack. This made him the first store owner at Carrolwood Mall to close up shop. After taping a sign to the metal security gate – *We Will Return When Gravity Does* – we boxed up stuff to take home. "For safekeeping," he said, though this didn't explain the unpacked inventory: the headphones and batteries and smart phones. When I asked why he'd ordered new stuff, he said, "I tried to predict what we might need at home." On Sunday at noon, he told me I could call it a day, but not before handing me fifty dollars for helping out. Some of this money made it only as far as the food court. The rest went with me to Game Addiction at the mall's far end. A lot of aliens died that afternoon.

One of the things Dad took home from the store was a complete ham radio kit. Later that week, I helped set it up. Even before we had finished, it took up the narrow end of our living room and could have been mistaken for an old entertainment center with one of those huge black receivers they used to sell in thrift stores. It even looked like it had speakers on each end. These were the bulky back-up battery packs that rose from the floor.

"Food's not the only thing that's going to be scarce," he said while plugging the unit's thick black cord into the power strip.

"Power, water, communication… enjoy them now."

Adding, "Here goes nothing," he clicked on the unit and lifted the round black microphone close to his mouth. "They call this keying it up."

A few seconds passed. We heard static, voices.

"Greetings from Carrolwood, Florida. Suburb north of Tampa," Dad said. "We are the Weavers. New kids in town." He sat in the extra wooden chair from our kitchen table set. He could easily have chosen something more comfortable for his official ham chair, like the recliner or couch. But from what I was seeing, he took his new role seriously. Relaxing wouldn't be part of it. As I watched him then, he reminded me of a ship's captain. Dad at the helm.

"Welcome, Weavers," a man's deep voice answered. "Alaska here. If we lived in the Lower Forty-Eight, I know where we'd be headed. We'd find a way."

"NASA's Ark?" Dad said. "What can you tell us about it?"

"That seems to be the big question these days," Alaska replied. "My wife likes to say it's the one topic that makes ham time unboring. Gravity's not coming back, no matter how hard they try to convince us otherwise. And that's got a lot of us believing there really is an office building fitted to work as a space station. It will lift off on its own the moment we hit True Zero G. 'Course, if the Ark exists, the next question is, where the heck is it? Most Arkies say Washington, but some say Texas, and others Virginia. Then there's that other big question. Who makes it onboard? How important do you have to be? They're sure not giving out passes to folks out here in the hinterlands."

A gray scratchy voice made me think of smoke from a campfire. "There's no way no one's getting on no Ark. There's ten different guesses on where it might be, and ten different reasons to believe there ain't even one to begin with. Like lemmings to a cliff, that's all it is. See how they run."

Dad looked annoyed. "Alaska, are you still there?"

"Pentagon. Anti-gravity experiments." The strange scratchy voice had not finished. "Higgs boson. God Particle. You mess with the fabric of the universe, it might just unravel."

When Alaska rejoined the conversation, it was to say, "Stranger things have happened. I truly believe the government's got an Ark. And if there's an Ark, there's a way to get on it."

The scratchy voice took issue with this. "Yeah right, if you're some Howard Hughes billionaire. Haven't you heard, the meek inherit the Earth? It's just no one told us it wouldn't be worth mosquito droppings."

The longer I listened to the debate that followed, the more I agreed with Alaska's wife. Ham time wasn't boring. I also learned that the idea of NASA's Ark was hardly a new one to Dad. Not the way he slipped in questions. *"And where do you think it's located?...How many passengers is it supposed to accommodate?"* After he signed off, he shared a few thoughts he'd been saving for me: "You want to hear what I believe? All the politicians and scientists went into the Capitol Building, along with truckloads of supplies, right after the Call to Maintain." He spoke slightly faster than usual, the way he did when stuff seemed important to him. "They did this as a ruse to keep people away from the real Ark at NASA's Langley Research Center in Virginia. The VIP's were transported there after sneaking out of the Capitol. There are tunnels everywhere in Washington."

I heard enthusiasm, which didn't seem like a good thing right then. Did Dad believe, like the people on his ham, that gravity was about to disappear completely? "You're not thinking we should go?" I asked.

He waited a good five seconds. "I'd like to think the scientists are right and that gravity will come back."

"Then why build an ark?"

"Now that would be the question. The one thing we do know

for sure is they're not building it for us. Imagine the security, imagine the competition from everyone trying to force their way onboard. Gaining passage would be close to impossible." Dad shook his head and smiled uncertainly. "On the other hand, to quote our new friend, stranger things have happened."

CHAPTER FOUR

Something in the Air

When Mr. Gelb shouted, "Mind your own business, Weaver, I ain't gonna slip and fall skyward like some Cirque du Soleil freak-show acrobat," he turned out to be right. But only because our pinch-faced old neighbor was about to discover a whole new way to leave the Earth.

It was a Tuesday morning, last week of June. Mr. Gelb stood on his roof dinking with a satellite dish. "Marion," Dad shouted from our carport, "that doesn't seem very wise. Do you want to float away?"

I stayed close to our car, the massive black Cadillac Fleetwood we had owned since Dad traded our two Hondas for it. I was waiting for him to unlock the doors, a process that required an actual key because the car was ancient, like 1962 ancient, which probably made it as old as Mr. Gelb. We were taking it to Newton, thirty miles east of Tampa, to bring Grammy back from the assisted living home she'd been in for five years. She had stopped communicating and couldn't be reached by phone or email. No one there could, prompting Dad to say it was time for action.

For what it was worth, the day couldn't have been more perfect. With no clouds coming in from the west, the sky was blue enough to be in a postcard. *Greetings from Sunny Florida. Wish You Were Here.* "Come on, Marion." My dad wasn't good at giving up. "A roof is no place to be." He didn't have to add that one slip could mean goodbye, up you go, even if you were wearing a stupid orange life preserver like Mr. Gelb was.

Our scrawny old neighbor acted like he couldn't hear. And after a while, he probably couldn't, not with two slim cyclones of churning debris appearing from nowhere. Just before Dad shoved me inside the door to our house, Mr. Gelb left his roof, shooting sideways toward the closest twister like metal to a magnet. I'm pretty sure it sucked him right in though I was indoors by the time that happened.

Dad stayed outside.

"Dad!" I pounded the window near the top of our door. He turned away just as a gust of wind knocked him sideways two feet. "Dad, no!" He bent down near his workbench to rescue the solar panels we planned to install out back. He picked up the top crate; the wind wrestled him for it, fighting to pry it free. Dad didn't let go, and almost went with it. When he gave up, he staggered backwards.

I leaned out the door to grab his shirt and pull him inside. Mom steered us the rest of the way, down the short hallway and into our front room. "I'll get you some water," she said. "Sit now, the both of you." The lights went dark the same instant our windows did. We could still see, if not so well. "What is this?" Dad asked. "Gelb didn't even have time to scream."

"Garbage Storms." Mom pointed at the black TV. "They're everywhere."

Pounding on walls, kicking at doors, they hit from all sides. The slim dark trashnadoes roared out of the gray, three... sometimes four at a time. Every so often, a soda can or plastic bag would linger at a window, pressed against the glass. A tire had us turning and ducking but it rolled past without coming inside.

We didn't talk much the first three days. The noise made it hard. But I knew what Mom, Dad, and Molly were thinking, mostly because it was all you could think. After watching the Earth turn into an out-of-control merry go round, throwing off riders as it picked up speed, had the weather turned psycho to finish the job? So what if our house had not budged. It was probably just waiting for the right-size twister.

Late that third night our window exploded. Molly screamed. The Garbage Storms now raged inside the bedroom she and I had been forced to share ever since Dad turned hers into a storeroom. Debris pelted my face and arms. I felt glass from the window, along with the sand and trash. Noise drilled through my eardrums: a freight train inches away. Nolab, our four-year-old dachshund who hardly ever barked, jumped around on my bed, yapping at the chaos. "Adam!" Molly shouted. "What happened to the ceiling?"

With a shaking right hand, I felt for the flashlight under my pillow. Pushing its switch, I aimed out and down. Three Barbie dolls stared back through the grainy, moving grayness, their eyes wide with terror. Pointing up, I was able to tell Molly, "Ceiling's still there."

The next thing I saw made me jerk backwards, banging my head on the wall. Rising like a mountain range behind the dolls, a real-life alligator faced left toward the broken window and away from our door. Molly screamed again. I stood on my bed as far back as possible, too scared to make a sound. Gators, I knew, could jump several feet.

But he didn't do much beyond blinking the one eye I could see. "He's still alive," I said. "But he sure isn't moving." I batted away a plastic water bottle that kept coming at me with the will of a mosquito. Dirt burned my eyes.

"He could," Molly shouted, and sure enough, the gator twitched. Which kept my heart pounding. "But he's closer to your bed than mine."

"Not funny."

The flashlight's beam rolled up and down his bumpy gray back. "At least he's not facing us." I held the light on his lime-green eye, split in two by the cold black slit. He didn't react to the brightness.

"I think he's dazed," I shouted at my sister. "We should bolt." But my feet seemed bolted in place. They didn't want to be on the floor.

Poking through a crack in our door – and into the churning debris – a second flashlight created its own jittery comet trail.

"Dad!" Molly shouted.

I bent down to pick up Nolab. "Quiet, boy, quiet." The dog squirmed but didn't bark. "We don't need him looking up here."

"Is that… an alligator?" Dad said as Molly and I ducked our heads and shot through the angry cloud. He yanked us to safety, the two of us at once, then pulled the door shut with all his strength to seal out the gator and trash.

I tried to say thanks. No words came out. I felt Mom's arms, the tightest hug ever. It turned out to be the longest one, too.

"Are you alright?" Dad asked.

"Sure," I replied, though of course I was not, since "alright" was something none of us would ever be again.

Dad told Mom he'd find some sheets so that Molly and I could sleep on the couch and recliner.

But no one even wanted to sleep. That would have meant lying back down. We sat in the kitchen, our faces hollow and ghostlike in the glow of a single flashlight. Hardly anyone talked, and when we did, it was only to say something super lame, like how it would be light soon, or good thing Dad closed our bedroom door.

He got up from the table to fetch some snacks from the kitchen. "Might as well eat while were awake," he said, returning with bags of Cheese Nips and Chips Ahoy cookies. "We need to keep Maintaining." I wasn't sure this was true anymore. Not with a gator stuck in our house and trashnadoes raging outside.

He must have sensed what the rest of us were thinking. "This isn't the end," he said. "For all we know, this is the turning point. We bottom out here and gravity rebounds."

As Molly and I grabbed four cookies each, Mom wondered out loud if this wasn't the first-ever gator to visit Carrolwood. We didn't have swamps or creeks that close. You had to go over to Lutz if you wanted to see a gator.

"He's got to be the first one to fly here," I said.

"Well," Dad said. "I have a plan."

Though there wasn't any meat in our house, apart of course from us, we would tempt the gator out with snacks. Dad proposed a trail of Doritos, mingling two flavors in case the gator had something against either Cool Ranch or Nacho Cheese. We would place these on the floor, two chips every foot, straight down the hallway, through the front room, and out the front door.

He added a final step. A remote control toy, a small one he'd brought home from Radio Shack, would scurry from chip to chip. Movement, Dad said, was what attracted alligators to food. So long as the "Cyber Bug" could outrun the gator, we had our plan. "We'll have to wait for the storms to die down," he added, "and that could take a while. Since no one's witnessed a Garbage Storm before, it's hard to predict how long they last."

He looked over at Molly, whose eyes showed doubt – and whose cheeks puffed out like a nut-toting squirrel's. She was trying to chew two cookies at once. "They can't go on much longer," he said.

Willie – Dad had given the gator a name – didn't make much noise that first night. But when the sun came up to paint the chaos outside a slightly lighter gray, he thundered to life.

We heard him charging and crashing, as loud as the storm. At times he roared like a lion.

For two more nights, Molly and I slept in the front room, closing our eyes even less than we had in our beds. Trash still pounded the outside of our house, along with the inside of our bedroom. Willie kept making noise. He banged against walls. He found glass to break.

The storms ended midmorning, leaving the loudest silence ever. Without waiting for Dad to ask, I put Nolab in the bathroom where he wouldn't be mistaken for food. Dad arranged the bait. The Cyber Bug sat ready beside the first chip. When Dad opened the door to our room, Molly screamed, shocked by the wreckage. She screamed again when Willie jumped, his tail sliding like a snake as he turned to face us.

The gator seemed to take it all in, sniffing and looking around, and it was hard not to think he found us more tempting than the trail of Doritos. Standing on the couch, Mom, Molly, and I waved two baseball bats and a crowbar to make it clear we wouldn't go down easy. Half roaring, half groaning, Willie pointed his snout at the unarmed food. Dad tapped his remote. The Bug moved an inch. Willie did not. The Bug moved again. Willie waited.

As if to show us just how unimpressed he was, the gator closed his eyes. Then – maybe ten seconds later – the eyes slowly opened. He leapt at the Bug. We jumped too.

But Dad had been ready; the Bug skittered away. The first two chips were no longer there. Willie had found them and snatched it up quickly. Now, he seemed to take his time, judging the taste. A good two minutes passed. Willie blinked his eyes, and pounced on the Bug, gulping it down with the next chips.

Dad pulled a backup from his pants pocket. But he didn't need it. Willie was hooked on Doritos.

The gator made quick short leaps from chip to chip as if

they were sucking him forward. We still jumped each time he moved. Not that you could blame us. Stretching six feet from snout to tail, Willie was, in Molly's words, "the size of a school bus." His teeth were crooked and yellow but looked knife sharp. The one time he turned our way, we held our weapons out in front, banging them together. He thought for a second and resumed his journey.

After 32 chips, he made the final lunge onto our porch. Dad jumped forward with gator speed to slam the door. He even turned the lock in case Willie knew how to use doorknobs.

From our front window, we watched him slink across the wild, dense grass that I had not mowed for two months, heading toward what used to be Mr. Gelb's front lawn.

"Well," said Dad as the gator disappeared behind the wide green spikes of our century plant, "we've had better guests."

The sky stretched out forever, a pale seamless blue. "Strange," Mom said. "It's still as can be. Like the weather just stopped." As for Willie the flying gator, we never saw him again, and you can bet we kept our eyes open wide whenever we went out front. He had become one more thing I'd seen the last of, like going to Game Addiction, or having my own room. Sometimes, when our house felt even smaller than usual and I was wishing we could go someplace we no longer went, I imagined the cool grass sliding across my belly as I crossed a fresh lawn. I saw the look of terror in the black eyes of squirrels, as surprised to see an alligator as two kids had been when I crashed through their bedroom window. The sun felt good on my back. So did my afternoon naps. But I was running out of time. I needed to find water; I needed my home. I wanted the world I used to know.

CHAPTER FIVE

The End of History: A History

By late July, when the president gave his last TV address, half the country had gone Stone Age. Their power plants no longer worked. They couldn't recharge phones or microwave popcorn. We weren't in that half. Three days after the Garbage Storms stopped, the employees of Tampa Electric had returned to work, enough of them at least.

The president's appearance was super strange. A single camera framed him from a distance and seemed to deliberately blur his image. My sister thought they had placed a full glass of water directly in front of the lens. This seemed pretty imaginative on her part, until I started thinking she was right. The image was that distorted. Like maybe the president didn't want us to see how bloated he looked from Maintaining. Or as Mom suggested, because he wasn't really fat, and had been taking other measures than the one he'd prescribed for everyone else.

"Let us begin with a silent prayer," The president said, "for all the skinny people who floated away because they didn't heed my Call to Maintain." He then stayed silent a good three seconds, not much time for a prayer meant to cover so many people.

"My fellow Americans, I come before you tonight to bury these scurrilous rumors of military research gone awry. You have my personal assurance there have been no D.O.D. experiments in Gravity Alteration. All rumors of so-called attempts to locate and isolate the anti-graviton particle are categorically false. The particle exists only in theory, and we've had no luck proving that its opposite, the more fundamental graviton boson-2 particle, is anything more than some scientist's fantasy. These things aren't real, and even if they were, your government would never waste trillions of dollars trying to exploit their existence, not even in a well-meant bid to attain lasting SMP... sorry, Strategic Military Superiority. So please rest assured there are no tears in the fabric of the universe, and certainly none that bear our fingerprints."

We didn't wait for him to finish before going online to become even more baffled by the GB-2 Field and how it supposedly held everything together. "Stress-energy tensors?" I read aloud, looking over Dad's shoulder. "Electroweak symmetry?"

"There is light at the end of the tunnel," the president declared from our front room. "The Drop Down is reversing."

"Listen to him," said Mom. "He's like a broken iPod. You can press Shuffle all you want. He keeps playing the same tired song."

"Sorry, honey." Dad looked up from the laptop. "But you sound like one of the conspiracy theorists I keep hearing on the ham. I've got to believe what the president said. There's light at the end of the tunnel."

"Until gravity returns at full strength," President Lodeswirth continued, "we need to remain calm. It's what we as Americans do in times of crisis. We also need to keep Maintaining."

"Four score and seven boxes of Twinkies ago," Mom said. "He's just lucky he doesn't face re-election." This was something I'd heard her say before. Like when the president vetoed legislation to place safety nets all across America, twenty feet off the ground. Or when he killed plans to bury pipes just below the Earth's surface, to hold down magnetic boots, which would have been issued by the Department of Homeland Security. The president had called these proposals "budget busters" while insisting the Drop Down was temporary. "We can't just throw money at every little problem. Why not simply empty Fort

Knox, give everyone gold bars to put in their pockets?"

He ended his speech by promising, "Power will soon be restored to the 31 states currently without it." This was five more states than we had last heard. "Even California," he tried making a joke, "and we know how they voted in the last election. God bless the United States of America, all of them. And God speed the Drop Down's reverse."

We lost our power in the middle of August. That was when civilization pretty much crumbled around us. Mobs looted any building that might have food in it, from warehouses to produce stands to pet supply stores. Doctors abandoned hospitals. Cops called it quits. Fleeing guards left their prisons on permanent lockdown.

We stayed indoors to avoid what Dad described as "the people who own guns using them on each other." Mom painted a black zero with a slash through it – the government's way of saying, "Nobody's home" – on the front of our house. No one to mess with. No food to steal. If there were other survivors nearby, we didn't see them. Their windows smashed out by the Garbage Storms, the houses around us seemed empty. Mrs. Dunn's Kia Optima still sat in her driveway, but at an angle, its windshield gone. An old El Camino across the street had fared even worse. A birdhouse on a metal pole, thrust like a spear by the winds, had pierced the cab from side to side.

If there were others in our area, we didn't hear them on the ham. As far as Dad knew, there was only one other contact in all of Florida. Living in Key West, she had given him a firsthand account of the looting, saying she barely got home alive. "It doesn't mean I haven't talked with other survivors in our state," Dad explained one afternoon when I joined him by the ham. "A lot of these folks volunteer little in the way of location or history. They fear for their own safety. And you've got to assume there are millions more toughing it out who didn't think to get a radio or secure a backup power source when there was still time."

The last day of August, we cut off our hair. Except for Molly. She didn't care that without running water there would be no showers or shampoos, or as she put it, "Nobody's touching my hair!" Mom used a handheld razor to shave me and Dad right down to the scalp. Then he helped trim hers real short, using a pair of scissors. While he was going at it, I stared at the back of his head and the folds of skin he didn't used to have. It looked like pie dough would look if you squished it together and plopped it in a sink where a grown man had shaved. Poor Dad. He had never been heavy before. Of everyone in our family, he worked hardest to survive the Drop Down. Eating non-stop didn't come easily for him, especially compared to me and Molly who had never been shy about asking for seconds, even when our lives had not depended on it. Dad was the one who needed to think he was doing this for a reason, a big one. Like the future of his family.

I turned to see Molly staring at me. "Your head doesn't have any dents or scars," she said. "That's probably good since you're already ugly enough."

Once the panic lifted, which had a lot to do with the panicky themselves lifting off, Dad let us go outside, and not just for our bathroom breaks. This was our reward for Maintaining so successfully. But even with Mom stuffing the linings of our jackets with sand, we still felt safer when crammed inside. Being outdoors could be kind of spooky, the way you never ran into other people or heard the smallest sound. No crickets chirped. No tires squealed.

When it got dark, it got *dark*.

We tried telling ourselves how lucky we were to have so much food. But we had only the stuff Dad bought at Costco. This had all come from the snack and candy aisles. The canned goods were gone when he got there, snatched by the hoarders ahead of him, the ones, he said, who owned their own trucks.

Making it worse, the rules for Maintaining had changed. The world was losing gravity faster than we could make up for it. So instead of eating to keep our body weights steady, we ate as often as we could to simply slow the loss, trying to hold onto 100 pounds, then ninety, then...

By October, I had come close to doubling in size. On a Tuesday morning toward the middle of that month, a plump round face supported by a body as wide as the virtual pinball machine I once played at the mall stared back at me from the full-length mirror in Mom and Dad's bedroom. Stepping onto Mom's scale, I lowered my eyes and leaned forward to see the bold red ꟻ0.

I found Dad where I knew I would, in the front room, seated directly in front of the ham radio set-up. This had become our last connection to the outside world. It was our Internet, TV, and phone.

CHAPTER SIX

Countdown

"Hours, days..."

Words flowed in and out of the static like glimpses of taillights in a serious downpour.

"Gravity..."

"Going fast..."

Dad sat in his wooden chair.

"I'm down six more pounds," I told him.

"The Drop Down is picking up speed," he said.

He held the microphone close to his mouth. "Are you still reading me, Alaska?"

"Ten-four," a man's deep voice broke through the wall of noise. "It's getting harder, that's for sure."

A woman spoke, her words barely piercing the static: "Michigan here. If anyone's going, go now. Things changing fast. Fluctuations."

Dad barely got out his "How fast?" before she exclaimed, "Good Lord! I'm watching the RV lift off right outside our window! Twenty-two tons dry-weight it was! Rising straight up!"

Alaska weighed in: "Florida, if you're going to find that Ark, I'd say you'd best go now."

Dad clicked off the ham. "Adam, could you get your mother and sister?" He slowly got up from his seat. "We need a family meeting." Usually, this struck me as funny, since you couldn't move two feet in our house without bumping into another family member. But at that moment, it seemed pretty important.

I found Molly reading. Some book about horses. Mom was out back, airing out clothes, the closest she got to washing them in a world without electricity or running water. The sweatshirts and pants drooped lazily from the clothesline that stretched from carport corner to fence. A pair of Dad's boxer shorts stuck out sideways, while several socks pointed more upward than out. We had three other clotheslines that rarely got used. Installing these in June, Dad had called them lifelines. He told us to stay close to them when walking out back.

With her head tilted back, Mom stared at the sky. When I told her about the meeting, she didn't turn to face me. "It's over," she whispered at last. "No one's ever outrun the truth. It's time we stopped trying, time we stopped lying to ourselves."

"I don't know," I said. "I think Dad might have something different in mind."

I almost thought I heard her laugh, but knew it couldn't have been that. More like a sigh or nervous cough. "I'm sure he does," she said quietly. "I'm sure he does."

CHAPTER SEVEN

The Family Meeting

"The Drop Down," Dad said as we took our places at the kitchen table. "It's accelerating."

"I lost nine pounds since last week," Mom said between mouthfuls of Cheetos. "A year ago, I would've loved it." She and Dad were facing each other. I sat to Mom's right, directly across from Molly. Between us and the dark wood table, we filled the small room. Nolab, our now double-wide dachshund, stayed under the table. He couldn't do much else, stuck as he was between eight fleshy legs the circumference of pancake stacks.

Dad held out his chocolate-chip pretzel roll as if it were some kind of prop. "Zero G," he said, "is going to hit much sooner than anyone's been telling us."

"So what do we do?" Mom asked through orange lips that matched the tips of her fingers. "There doesn't seem much point in Maintaining. Not if we're nearing the end."

I gulped down a handful of candy orange slices. They tasted sweet though not half as much as they used to when I wasn't required to eat them. My sister leaned back in her chair, bumping its top rail against the wall. She seemed to be eyeing the crumbs on our ceiling that formed a dark sand desert broken up by sugar oases and perfectly round tents (brown M&Ms tossed up there deliberately). It made no sense why some debris stayed while other spills slowly descended back to table or floor. Or maybe I should say it made no *more* sense than all the other strangeness that had taken over our world. A few larger objects settled there, too, like my sock on the bedroom ceiling. Only the week before, I had to get Nolab down for a second time. He'd been chasing a palmetto bug and jumped. The palmetto bugs liked our ceilings for their sanctuary and crumbs, and Nolab, plump as he was, weighed next to nothing. Getting stuck up there was one of the few things that could make him bark. I could still see his terrified eyes looking down at me, pleading for help.

"I might have a solution. A real one." Dad's pretzel roll glistened. He liked dipping his food in honey. "By glum or by chum…" He looked around the table, pausing on each of our faces. "We are going to NASA's Ark. When it leaves the ground, the Weaver family will be on it." He was looking at me when he said, "We can't just stay here, stay here and…"

Molly gave him a few seconds before adding, "Lift up?"

"Yes, Pumpkin," he whispered. "Lift up."

A bead of honey rolled slowly down his chin, the first of three it had to cross. He took a napkin from the table, jerking it from under the brick that held the stack in place. After wiping his chins, he let go of the soft wadded paper. With a finger, he flicked it, while mouthing the word, "Liftoff." We watched it hang in the air.

"So many people," he sighed. "Already gone. They gave up, most without admitting it. We're not those people. We're still here, feet on the ground. We survived the Garbage Storms. We survived the Food Riots. And we're getting on the Ark."

Mom shook her head and smiled, which somehow made her look sadder. "How do you even know there is an Ark?" she asked. "The president denies it. We heard that from you."

"That's true," Dad said. "He's never changed that tune. But NASA's Ark is real. I'm sure of it."

"Even if you're right," Mom asked, "how would we sneak past whatever's left of the military?" She raised her left hand and raked the air with her fingers, waving them slowly past her neck. If I hadn't seen this before, I wouldn't have known she was trying to run those fingers through the long brown hair that used to be there. "How would we chip through the layers of concrete? And what's after that? Convincing the president that life can't go on without the Weaver family gene pool?"

Dad waited a few seconds before speaking. "I already started organizing supplies for going. Weeks ago."

"You what?"

"I got fed up. I hit my breaking point." Dad surprised us by raising his voice. "That's what I did. I couldn't just sit around grazing like some cow, watching the trucks pull up outside our stalls."

"You're shouting."

"I am not…" He stopped, breathed in and out slowly, then resumed with slightly less volume. "Shouting." He looked at Mom with pleading eyes. "After all we've been through… all we've put ourselves through…"

"But," Mom said, "you planned all this without saying a word? That's never been how this family works."

"I prepared," Dad said. "There's a difference. Like everyone else, I wanted to believe the Drop Down would level off. It just got harder and harder to make that leap."

He scratched his middle chin, something he did when he was nervous or weighing decisions. "I have a plan."

"There'll be hordes of desperate people," Mom said. "You're not the only one with a ham radio." She looked down at her hands and sighed. "I don't know. It seems impossible. Crazy."

"Staying put would be crazy." Still drifting over the table, Dad's napkin started to rise. He looked past it at Mom. "There's only one thing we really know. One single thing. Gravity is disappearing, and fast."

"Ark or no Ark," Mom said, "if we're really thinking of

going somewhere, I say we choose someplace nice. Someplace filled with memories and beauty."

"And where exactly is someplace nice?" Dad leaned across the table, as much as he could, to retrieve the runaway napkin. "You're not forgetting the past six months?"

"The beach, that's where. I want to drift off looking down on the spray and the sand. We used to go there, you might recall, before you spent all your time at the store. Maybe as I go up, I'll see both coasts, the Gulf and Atlantic. Instead of screaming in fear, I'll make myself hold onto that goal."

Dad looked like he was thinking – and having a hard time with it. "Well, of course," he said at last, "everyone loves the beach. But to just give up? That wouldn't be right."

"Whatever direction we choose to travel," Mom said, "we still reach that point where reality wins out."

"Giving yourself to the sky." Dad's voice got loud again. "It's not a good way to die. The only point you reach there is when your body explodes from the pressure."

I looked over at my sister, who seemed ready to cry.

"They don't all say that," Mom shot back. "Many believe you pass out first from shock and lack of oxygen, before the effects of ebullism."

"Right," said Dad, "and fairies will serenade us."

"I'm just quoting people who actually studied this stuff."

"Stop!" Molly cried.

Mom looked at her. "I'm sorry, Moll. But this could be the biggest decision we ever make as a family. Your dad and I both want what's best for everyone, and right now, we just can't agree."

"You never fight. Hardly ever."

"I keep forgetting," Mom said. "I've been saving something for you." She got up and went to the supply room that used to be our laundry room. When she returned, she was holding a photo book of *The World's Favorite Kittens*. Molly smiled and took the book.

"That looks like a wonderful book," Dad said as Mom sat back down.

Watching Molly to make sure she'd been fully distracted, Mom quietly said, "I don't want to spend my final hours fighting an impossible battle."

"We made it six months," Dad pleaded. "We don't just quit."

"Oh, please," said Mom. "I know I'm not the only one who thinks the beach makes more sense."

"And I can't be the only one who wants to hang on." Dad still looked confused and unhappy, like a guy in a fight, stunned by a punch to the head. This kept me from saying that, except for the part about just giving up, Mom's beach sounded good. I imagined the blinding sunshine reflections, split into ribbons by advancing waves. But then I wondered if we'd see waves at all. With the moon getting farther away, there were no tides. What did that mean for basic waves? Would the ocean still be loud? Would it seem like a movie where things moved and made noise? Or would it be like the world outside our house, silent and still like a photograph?

These questions made me curious. They made me want to see the ocean.

"When the Ark lifts off," Dad said, "you'll see the ocean. You'll see the whole world. We don't have to give up."

Nolab whimpered, almost inaudibly.

"Adam," said Mom, "I think your dog needs a fence break."

Dad persisted. "Our decision?"

"Dog peeing indoors?" countered Mom.

I got up from my seat and walked the few feet to our back door with Nolab trailing behind. Bending down, I fastened the Velcro on his double sandbag harness.

"I know what I'm proposing sounds like some impossible

quest," Dad said. "But can anyone name a single thing we've got to lose?"

"I don't know," Mom said weakly, "the last crumbs of reality?"

"Look around," he said. "This is unreality. You can hardly say we'd be risking our lives. We haven't seen anything resembling a life for six months now."

"All the more reason to go someplace nice."

I snapped on Nolab's leash. "If we're not willing to take this chance," Dad said, "I put our odds at nothing... zero in one hundred. We have nowhere to go but up."

Molly and I groaned.

"Kids," he said, "this is the most serious decision you're ever going to make. Don't make it your last one. Some thinking is required."

Molly grabbed a clump of her reddish brown hair, and used it to wipe her mouth. "What happened to everything just getting back to unmessed up? They said it would stop. They said gravity would come back."

Like me, Molly had inherited Mom's soft round face and plain brown eyes that always seemed to be asking questions, simple ones, like "Could you help tie my shoes?" Mom had been pretty when she was young; I knew this from a framed photo on her dresser. Taken when she was in college, it was literally the picture of innocence, of eyes that were hopeful and sweet. A boy like Dad would never have known what he was up against. Those eyes hid Mom's super tough intelligence. Unlike Molly's which weren't hiding much.

The only thing I got from Dad was my dark, thick hair, which sure didn't seem fair, and not just because of shaving it off. Of the four people squeezed into our house, Dad had come closest to having TV actor looks. Women at the mall stopped by his store to talk; they sure never bought anything. This probably would have worried Mom if Dad's eyes weren't just a little too close together, or his smile less forced. He never gave the impression he knew how to relax.

"I'm sorry, Pumpkin," he said now, reaching over to touch Molly's shoulder. "But they were only a few scientists to begin with."

"And the president!" she reminded him.

"They were just trying to keep us in our homes," he said. "I think we know that now."

"Molly, Adam, your father's right. You should take some time and think. Think about the difference between looking out on a shimmering blue horizon, and fighting who knows what on some impossible quest."

I heard Dad say, "We can beat this, I know it," as I went out the door. "Hope is not the worst thing to have."

CHAPTER EIGHT

With Dog as My Witness

Nolab scurried to the tall wooden fence, his belly gently dragging the whole way. Our fence had become the bathroom – and not just for the dog, since the indoor versions weren't flushing so well. We each had our own section.

Nolab moved quickly, which was one of the stranger things about Low G. As big as we'd grown, we could move faster than ever before because we weighed so little. Of course, we also wore out faster, thanks to our size and the thinning supply of atmosphere. By Dad's math, we had each added eighty miles of new blood vessels, enough to stretch from Tampa to Orlando, in making our bodies bigger.

Watching Nolab scuttle like a cockroach surprised by kitchen lights always reminded me just how "alternate" our universe had become. After all, in Nolab's case, he had not just been *known* for taking life slow. He had been *named* for it. Four summers ago, I wanted a Labrador retriever who could fetch rubber bones and bark at people I didn't like. Specifically, I wanted the Black Lab named Rocky we found on tampalabrescue.org. Dad shot this down fast, contending that our house and yard were way too small for a way big dog. I could not have the Lab.

I was still exercising my right to complain the day we went to the animal shelter. But secretly, I had as much fun as Mom, Molly, and Dad picking out our dachshund, which proved easier than finding a name for him. Though "Oscar" and "Roland" outlasted Molly's "Weiner Boy," neither really took hold. Sometimes he was Oscar, and sometimes he was Roland. The dog showed himself to be very loving, especially toward his food, but he couldn't learn a trick no matter how many Milk Bones were dangled just outside his reach. Each time we tried getting Oscar or Roland to fetch his green ping-pong ball, he would scamper a few yards before stopping like some old grandpa whose grandkids had worn him out. At which time I would say, "He's no Lab." Molly quickly picked this up and repeated it to death, even when the poor dog had not just given up on a trick. It didn't take long for "no Lab" to become Nolab.

Stopping parallel to the fence, he lifted a leg and aimed, as always missing his target. The golden arc curved upward before painting its tall slender oval on the wooden slats, level with my shoulders. Pleased with his effort, he shook, his bloated body going every which way. I thought of some kittens I'd seen online, wrestling under a blanket – a comparison he wouldn't have liked.

"So, boy, how am I supposed to vote?"

Nolab tried to scratch his ear, though his hind legs no longer got close enough. Missing by a good three inches, he looked like he was waving goodbye.

"It's been a long time since I've been to the beach," I said. "But I remember. You'd like it." We walked alongside the fence. He stopped to sniff the circle on the ground where Molly's plastic kiddie pool sat before it became a blue flying saucer during the Garbage Storms. "But I've never had an adventure. Not really. And Dad's idea… it sure wouldn't be boring."

All I really knew for sure was that something had to give. Dad was right about that: we had nothing to lose, including what Mom called the last crumbs of reality. Because unless you really loved sitting around and shoveling down Pringles and reading books you'd already read, our reality ranked right down there with being a Roman slave or telemarketer.

Looking around, as Dad had suggested, could really depress you. We lived in a house half prison, half warehouse. It didn't matter that we owned computers and TVs and other cool crap. None of it worked. Dad wouldn't let us use any of the half-million batteries he'd hoarded away. These, he said, were for backing up the ham radio. And flashlights.

And so Molly read about horses and royal weddings and star-crossed romances she would never get to experience. I pored over my sci-fi novels. Almost all of them foretold some kind of doomsday, like nuclear winter, or mutant snakes, or robot invasions, which left me feeling cheated, since none of these doomsdays could happen now.

Nolab stopped to pee again.

"I don't know about you, boy," I said. "But I think I could use the adventure."

I swore I heard clanking from the Dunn house next door, empty now a good three months. But looking at the windows, all I saw was the sun's blinding glare.

Nolab wandered that direction. But it wasn't the sound that lured him. It was some smell on the ground, one he'd probably sniffed a hundred times before. "Okay now, okay. Time to go back in." We started back. He led the way. I glanced at the reflective silver tarp that covered our water tank and noticed a loose bungee cord. This was our backup tank, but with the main tank close to empty, our lives would soon depend on it. "One minute," I said while bending down to hook Nolab's leash to the hitching post Dad had installed in the middle of our yard. "Wait here."

But before I could finish, the concrete bench by the house lifted from the ground, advancing quickly from knee high to eye level to "there it goes." As it rose above the trees, the birdbath took chase, leaving a dead brown circle where it had been sitting.

"Zero G," I whispered while lifting Nolab. "For real."

Soon nothing more than a dot in the sky, the birdbath had probably saved my life by warning me the Zero G pocket was either growing or moving. I knew I couldn't stay put. Facing our back door, I leaned forward, ready to run. With one last deep breath, I became our school's star quarterback, charging toward the goal line with a Nolab football tucked firmly under my arm.

Passing close to where the bench had been, I felt a strange lightness. My feet left the ground. But the momentum carried me forward. I hit the house just above the backdoor.

My breath roared and heart pounded. But I was able to whisper, "Nolab, we made it." I pushed against the eaves with my free arm and sank slowly to the ground.

CHAPTER NINE

Democracy InAction

"Adam, what is it?" Mom asked as I slammed the door behind me. "You look like you just saw the Grim Reaper. And why are you holding the dog?"

"We had to run through a patch of Zero G to get back inside!"

Dad took a few seconds to process this.

"Zero G?" he said. "In our backyard? Close to the house or back by the fence?"

He didn't let me answer. "This just proves we need to move fast," he said. "NASA's Ark will rise up soon. If we're to have any chance of surviving this—"

"Or going to the beach," Mom added.

"That's what I want," Molly said. "I'm sorry, Dad, but getting on a building that turns into a spaceship? That's more crazy than the stuff in Adam's books." Using her left hand, she played with her hair. Her right hand clutched a box of multi-colored Goldfish crackers.

"Adam?" said Mom.

Nolab squirmed, reminding me to set him down.

As weird as it seemed, Molly's words had made sense. Our getting aboard the mysterious NASA's Ark was harder to swallow than a third bag of Doritos. I took a deep breath and walked to the table. "I like the beach."

"Yes, yes," said Molly.

"The sun and the sand," I continued, "the wide blue sky and

endless sea. But I think we should go to NASA."

"Adam," said Dad, "have you been listening—" He stopped and smiled, looking at me in honest-to-God wonder.

"That's right, Dad. I'm agreeing with you." I took my seat to his left.

"Is that the tally?" Mom said. "Two for Dad's fantasy, and two for the beach?"

Molly belched, then went back to chewing. Somebody farted – Dad or the dog.

"We need to give this more thought," Dad said. "We can't have a split vote."

"There's no split vote," said Mom.

"What do you mean?" Dad asked.

"The windmill chase wins. We're not going to waste our final hours fighting."

"These won't be our final hours."

"And that's not the point," Mom said. "Whatever the road, we go as a family. Together."

"Maybe," I suggested, "we aim for NASA and if that doesn't work, we find a nice beach."

Molly raised her hand like she was in school. "Can we stop and get Grammy?"

This caused some serious silence.

"Pumpkin," Dad finally said, "we were ready to get her weeks ago. But the Garbage Storms came, the Food Riots broke out, it just didn't seem safe. I'm sorry, but I think we missed our window on that one."

We heard three loud knocks. Someone at our door.

None of us spoke. The knocking grew louder.

Pushing himself up from his chair, Dad tried making a joke, "Anyone expecting a UPS delivery?" He sounded nervous.

"I don't think we should answer that," Mom said.

CHAPTER TEN

Like a Dream, Only Different

The pounding got louder. Whoever stood outside our door, he sure wanted something.

Nolab scuttled out from under the table, looked toward the front room, and ran down the hall, away from the danger. The sound of his nails clacking on wood made me think of Mom at her laptop, back when things weren't so messed up, typing furiously in response to Facebook posts by a cousin who disagreed with her about our president's qualifications. (Mom didn't think he had any.)

"Dad," I whispered, motioning toward the brick that secured our paper napkins. But he didn't take it to use as a weapon.

I followed him to the front room.

"You stay back, Adam. We don't know who – or what – is out there."

And that, I thought, looking down at the brick in my hand, *is why you should be the one wielding this.*

Dad yanked open the door, and there stood Kylie Cho, one of the popular girls from school. She looked tiny in her blue-gray Asteroids cheerleader uniform, tiny because she hadn't gained weight, choosing instead to wear actual weights like some freak-show fashion accessory.

I saw two kinds, starting with the strap-on ones that runners once used. Held in place by Velcro strips, they zebra-fied her arms and lower legs. But these were nothing compared to the round cast-iron plates in a variety of sizes. *10LB. 25LB. 50LB.*

Silver-gray bands of duct tape, fully circling her waist and chest, held these discs in place, while making me think she probably hadn't changed her plain gray T-shirt in some time. She wore no weights on her upper legs, probably so she could go to the bathroom, which was tricky enough nowadays without adding obstacles. Her black running shorts had silver stripes on the sides.

"She's skinny," Molly whispered.

"Hi," Kylie said shyly, a real change from her thunderous pounding. "Adam? How have you been?"

"Okay, I guess." I might have come up with a cleverer answer had Kylie Cho ever once talked to me before. I'd only ever known her as the cheerleader girlfriend of Q, the bully jock behind "Adam, Adam, four by eight." I had always tried to hate her. But my brain didn't go along.

Dad was looking at me. "This is Kylie Cho," I said. "She went to my school."

"We knew that some people survived without Maintaining," Dad noted while scratching his middle chin. "We just didn't know any had held on this long. You want to come…"

She charged past him before he reached the "in?"

Strange, but I couldn't shake my reaction that Kylie looked scrawny. I sure wouldn't have thought this eight months before, but that was true for a lot of thoughts. I did like it that she still wore her hair long. Molly did too, of course, but hers just looked stupid because she knew better than to keep it long and impossible to clean.

Not that I could ignore how Kylie's hair had lost its brilliant sheen, one more thing to blame on the absence of healthy stuff like protein in our food. I still thought it looked cool, darker than black, like night had become without moonlight or electric power.

"Well," said Dad, "welcome to our home."

"Thanks." Kylie held her hand to her throat. "I think I need to sit down."

Dad offered her his recliner. "Molly," he said, "could you get our guest some water and crackers?"

Nolab came out of the kitchen to growl at Kylie, which hit me as super strange since Nolab never growled at anyone or anything.

"Well," said Dad.

Ignoring Nolab's rudeness, Kylie did something even stranger. She pulled a phone that looked way too big to be a phone out of a belt clip that looked more like an Old West holster. The phone was so big it reminded me of phones in really old movies from when Mom and Dad were growing up. But what was Kylie doing with it? She had to know cell phones needed satellites and service providers to work.

"Impressive walkie-talkie," Dad quelled these thoughts. "It looks like a professional model. Meant for long distances."

"Yeah, cool walkie-talkie," I quietly added.

When Molly returned, the rest of us took seats on the couch and chairs.

Kylie devoured a cracker. "My family," she began, shooting crumbs out with the f. "They didn't plan well." Her crumbs rose toward the ceiling. "They started out denying the crisis."

"Deniers." Dad smirked. "They used to be everywhere, starting with the president."

"And ending with my parents," Kylie said. "They got a late start. Like two months late. It took watching my aunt get swept away in a Garbage Storm. Gone. In this great big swirl of trash and plastic bottles."

"There weren't many Deniers after the Garbage Storms," Dad noted.

"Pa filled up our freezer and two refrigerators, the one in our kitchen and one in our carport. He was fighting the Drop Down.

But he never gave much thought to the power going out."

I lost track of her story for a bit, my thoughts straying to perishable food. I know it seems hard to believe you could hunger for something when you've been eating non-stop for six months. But all those refrigerated foods… the cookie dough… guacamole… cheese that didn't come from aerosol cans…

"My parents didn't last much longer than that." Kylie had my attention again. "They got carried off during the Food Riots."

We all nodded, remembering the time when everyone from Sunday school teachers to Olympic athletes became looters.

"We got in and out of the Super Wal-Mart with only a few minor scraps. We didn't even see any police. We'd gone there thinking we were prepared for anything, including Low G. We wore backpacks front and back, filled with big, hulking flagstones we took from our patio. We even tied ourselves together at the ankles. But right out front at the edge of the lot my folks hit a bubble of Zero G. They got caught off guard. You only get caught off guard once."

"Like Adam in the backyard," Molly said. "Only he didn't float off."

"Up they went," Kylie resumed without emotion, "wailing and screaming… and praying in a way that still sounded like screaming."

"What happened to the rope?" Molly asked. "Why didn't you lift off, too?"

"It was weird," Kylie said. "The rope tipped me over, but then pulled off. Took my shoe with it."

"What did you do after that?" Mom asked. "With your parents gone?"

"I managed to get their shopping cart back to the car, then taught myself to drive enough to get home. The food lasted exactly ten days. After that, I went to my boyfriend's house. Q. You probably remember him, Adam, strong and tough but kind of sweet. He was helping me unload my stuff when he tripped and floated away, all the while shouting I should keep right on going and not look back."

Kylie lowered her eyes to where skinny fingers tapped nervously, like they were typing on some invisible keypad and not just bony knees. "His family took me in. They were the ones who wrapped me in weights. Q's old set. They'd been Maintaining from early on. Looked like a pair of sumo wrestlers… gross."

I looked down at the floor, felt myself blushing.

"But just like my folks," Kylie resumed, "they were running low on food, especially non-perishables."

Molly said, "Our dad was smart about that. Right from the start he bought things up."

"It made no sense," Dad volunteered, "waiting to see if the Drop Down was 'an adjustment to get used to' as scientists said or a 'temporary thing' as the president said. I didn't need to see the power grid fail to know where this story was going."

"Q's family had to ration," Kylie resumed, "which meant they weren't gaining weight half as fast as they wanted. Finally, just a few weeks back, they called it quits."

"They gave themselves to the sky?" Molly said. This was the expression for rising up deliberately.

Kylie nodded. "They went outside and whispered to the dirt beneath their feet, 'Goodbye, cruel world.' Really, those exact same words. Then, just before they leapt to their deaths, they told me to keep the memory of their son alive. They wanted me to eat what was left of their food."

"And did you?" Dad asked.

She nodded. "Right up until the food ran out. Last couple of days I was hiding in the house next door to yours. Just watching and praying I'd see you in a window." Looking at me, she added, "Bet you never thought you'd have a stalker, Adam Weaver." She laughed, but only for a second. "I needed to make sure you'd survived. When I saw you out back, I tried getting your attention. The windows were sealed shut, but I banged on the glass. With both of my fists. You didn't seem to hear. You were playing weird games with your wiener dog."

As if in response, Nolab went back to growling.

"Adam?" Molly said. "Could you help me check the water tank cover outside? I'm not sure I tied all the tarps back down."

"I just saw it when I was out there. Except for one hook, it looked perfectly okay."

"We really need to check it," Molly said with more volume.

"I'm not so sure that's a good idea," Dad said. "It's not like Adam's patch of Zero G has warning flags around it."

"Molly, you put on your jacket," Mom said, meaning the one lined with sand. "And stay close to the house. It's dangerous out there."

"I'll hold onto the house rail," Molly assured her. Dad had installed these on the outside walls way back in June before we really needed them.

"No letting go," said the mom who had just been pushing for us to go to the beach and do exactly that.

"We'll be careful," Molly assured her.

"Maybe I should go," said Dad. But Molly and I were already at the door, with my sister pushing me forward.

"This better be important," I whispered.

CHAPTER ELEVEN

Shedding

I didn't even get the backdoor closed before Molly sputtered, "That cheerleader... her family... her boyfriend." She turned to face me, switching hands to keep hold of the house rail. "How come she's still alive and no one else is?"

"What are you saying?"

"Nolab never growls at anything."

"The same Nolab who hasn't seen a stranger in months?"

Molly turned back around and walked a few yards, staying close to the wall like she promised. "She never cried during her story. Not once ever."

She couldn't see me shaking my head.

"And what about the rope?" She stopped on the other side of our kitchen's bay window where Mom used to keep flowers. "Just magically slipping loose from her ankle?"

"Knots come loose."

She faced me again. "If she stays here," she continued, "we'll be next."

"She's hardly a killer."

"She's sure good at being the only one who doesn't die."

I tried to laugh, but nothing came out. "Even if your theory made sense," I said, "why would she want to hurt us?"

"Can't you see, Romeo? Our food."

"Romeo?"

Molly's eyes narrowed. "You think she's cute."

"She is cute. But that doesn't mean I like her."

"Like I believe that," Molly sneered. "You always liked the ones who didn't like you, instead of just talking to girls who were like you."

"Like you know more about girls and stuff than your brother who's almost in high school."

"It hurts, doesn't it?"

Something in the kitchen caught my attention: dozens of floating napkins, each a tiny magic carpet rising slowly to the ceiling. I must have disturbed the pile when I took the brick weight. "She's had bad luck," I said.

"Or maybe," said Molly, "she *is* bad luck."

I looked back to see Dad, who had probably come outside to make sure we were safe.

"I heard you, Molly," he said quietly. "Don't let your imagination get the better of you."

"I didn't imagine five people got killed. I didn't imagine Nolab growling."

"I don't see how anyone could be afraid of that scared, skinny girl," he said. "She can't weigh much more than Nolab. And even if she just wants our food, she's not going to kill us for it. Not if we're pulling up stakes in the morning. She can stay here and eat anything she wants when we're gone."

A blast of noise tore through the quiet, a loud crashing and screeching from the Dunn house where Kylie had been staying. Had she been alone or were there others? Some sort of Zombie Cheerleader Army?

But then I saw the source of the commotion: a metal Tuff Shed taking off. A white triangle tip appeared first, followed by the fake-shingle roof and finally, the whole creaking, wobbling structure.

A pair of squirrels trailed close behind, tumbling upward, tails totally puffed out, eyes wide and frantic. In between screeching, they made super-fast clicking sounds, like someone typing too loud in Computer Lab. "Flying squirrels," I whispered. "They must have been living in the shed." As Dad once said, you had to admire squirrels for their tenacity – and claws. It was how they'd put off extinction that long, clinging to life with sharp curled nails.

"Well," Dad whispered. "Another pocket of Zero G."

"You always hated their Tuff Shed," Molly noted. "Yuck!" she added with a shout, as a corpse floated up. Mrs. Dunn didn't look too good; the squirrels had found a source of food. Cringing, I looked away.

"Back inside, kids!" Dad shouted. "Hold onto the rail! From now on, no going out!"

"How will we go to the bathroom?" Molly asked as he pushed her along.

"The house can smell bad for one night."

"What was all that about?" Mom asked once we were back inside. "Sounded like all hell broke loose."

"More like a Tuff Shed," said Dad. "Things are definitely changing out there."

"Where's Kylie?" I asked.

"Where's Nolab?" Molly cried at almost the same time.

Mom smiled, a rare occurrence, as Nolab came out of the kitchen. "Everyone, calm down. Kylie's just getting her things from the porch."

I started toward the door to see if she needed help, but Kylie beat me there. She held a super-stuffed backpack – a big one, like campers used to carry – in one slender hand. Latched to the backpack were a two-gallon water jug and a black violin case.

"Need any help?" I asked, but she squeezed past me.

"Thought I better bring this in," she said.

I took a seat on the couch across from her.

Nolab growled quietly – inwardly. It sounded like an angry purr.

"What about our trip?" Molly said.

"A trip?" asked Kylie. "To where? There's nothing out there."

"NASA's Ark," Dad said a bit too excitedly.

"The Ark?" Kylie leaned forward, her eyes fixed on Dad. "Q's dad said something about that."

"It's not where everyone thinks," I said, trying to impress her.

"I didn't know it had room for regular people," she said.

"They're going to make room," Dad said.

"A lot of people built their own arks," Kylie said. "Using houses and airplanes."

Dad shook his head. "They won't last a week in space."

Kylie pulled her walkie-talkie back out, staring at it as if she could magically will it back to life.

"Why do you keep looking at that thing?" Molly asked. "You know there's nobody to talk to."

"Right around when it got impossible for the Deniers to keep denying, my grandpa got these for us. So we could talk to him if phones and stuff died. He was in that assisted-living place out east of town. Same as your grandma."

"He's still alive?" Molly asked.

"Not as far as I know," Kylie said. "He stopped calling some time back. But—" She paused like a thespian in one of our school plays, going for maximum drama. "Someone else got through."

Kylie looked at our faces, taking her time, and I could tell she enjoyed the power she held over us as storyteller.

"Who?" Molly spurted.

Kylie waited another five seconds before saying, "Your grandma."

"Grammy's still alive?" Molly squealed.

"She sounded that way when she was talking."

"When was that?" Dad said at the same time I asked, "What did she say?"

"Two days ago," Kylie replied. "This little, quavering voice: 'Could somebody tell the Weavers in Carrolwood I'm still alive? Could somebody tell my Bill? They need to get me out of here. This stink hole stank before the Drop Down, and it's only gone downhill since. Don't even ask what I've been putting in my mouth.'"

"That's Grammy all right," said Mom.

"Two days?" Dad said. "Are you certain?"

"Two days."

"Maybe I'm just used to hearing news that's too true to be good," he said. "But that's very hard to believe."

"We just assumed she was gone," Mom said. "Like all the others in assisted-living facilities. We talked about rescuing her when the power went out, but with all the riots and shootings, knew we couldn't get there."

Kylie shoved the walkie-talkie back in its holster. "It's what made me think of finding you, Adam. Remembering how you were always... you know, kind of big. I was hoping you were still alive."

She asked my father, "Are you Bill?"

"His father," Mom explained. "Kids' grandfather. He's been gone some time. Not unlike Grammy's memory."

"For the most part she's fine," Dad said. "It's just that some of the things she remembers never took place."

Nolab barked. *Get out of our house.* It came out of nowhere.

Kylie glared at Nolab. I looked over at Molly. Her "told you" smirk was every bit as hard to misread.

"Your dog's got some issues," Kylie said.

Molly reached down to try and pet him. "Dad says they're good judges of people."

CHAPTER TWELVE

Unsettling News

Molly wasn't happy to learn that Kylie was going with us. "Why can't she just stay in our house and eat the food we leave behind? She's not some stray dog Adam found in the park." Our family was huddled in Mom and Dad's bedroom, using up most of the space that wasn't actual bed.

"She's a human being who needs our help," Dad said.

A black palmetto bug the size of an Oreo cookie crawled across the ceiling looking for crumbs.

Molly sputtered, "This was Adam's idea, wasn't it?"

She was both right and wrong. It had been my idea, but I had been spared from saying so when Mom and Dad came up with it on their own. No one needed to know how I wanted to impress Kylie Cho with my courage and resourcefulness so that I could show her what a mistake she'd made with a boyfriend like Q. I knew it wasn't all that plausible, this fantasy of mine, but what did I have to lose?

"It's the right thing to do," said Dad. "It's—" His attention was hijacked by the music coming from our front room. As eerie as they were beautiful, the violin notes seemed to hang in midair the way our napkins had.

"Your friend?" Mom asked.

"I guess."

We walked to the front room, stopping just inside. Kylie blushed but kept on playing.

When she stopped a few minutes later, she said, "'Valse Triste.' Sibelius."

She didn't look so scrawny now, which meant I was getting used to thinness again.

Molly stared at her violin with a hard, suspicious look like she was trying to figure out a magic trick. "Why'd you waste time on being a cheerleader?"

"That's a hard one, Molly. Let me think. Oh, now I remember… *because I enjoyed it.*"

"You sounded amazing," Mom said as Kylie carefully placed her violin back in its case. "Really amazing. There was a time I hoped one of our brood would learn an instrument."

When I walked back to the bedroom I never had to share with Molly before this all started, I was surprised that Kylie followed me. Sliding her finger along the paperback spines of my sci-fi collection, she said, "*The Space Merchants.* Cool."

Holding it up in front of the heavy plastic sheet that served as our window, she told me she used to own dozens of eBooks. "My favorite authors, favorite stories, all gone in the blink of a power outage."

"These still work," I said. "So what else did my Grammy have to say?"

"Just what I told you," she replied. "I tried talking to her, tried asking some questions, but I don't think she could hear. These aren't the world's best walkie-talkies. Grandpa got them at Radio Shack."

"Don't let my dad hear that," I said, smiling. "He managed the one at the mall." Not that there was much danger of his overhearing. He had retreated to the carport, where he seemed intent on creating the most noise possible, hammering things and shoving things and using words that Molly and I got in trouble for using. You might have thought he was building his own Ark.

I led Kylie to the front room. She stretched out on the couch, taking advantage of the fading light to read a few chapters from *Oryx and Crake.* From back in my bedroom, I heard her laugh a few times. This was a good thing, even if Nolab growled quietly each time she did so.

Dad must have dug into his battery supply. His experiments with noise endured way into the night, meaning he had at least one flashlight out there. He was still going strong when I closed my eyes.

I couldn't know what time it was when Kylie screamed. It was a long, harrowing scream, a roller-coaster scream, and I woke up sure our house was lifting off. Reaching down, I clutched the bed's metal frame, as if that would somehow protect me.

CHAPTER THIRTEEN

Exit Signs

Our Cadillac Fleetwood was parked in the driveway. From where we stood inside the carport, we saw how much it had grown – eight feet overnight, more if you counted the antennae. The shadow it cast in the early morning sun stretched all the way to the Dunn house driveway. On top of its roof, our washer, dryer, and double-door fridge interlocked neatly like pieces in a puzzle, even if they stuck out a few extra feet on the front and sides. Red plastic cans of gas, suitcases, and old laptops filled the few spaces left. Dad's ham radio set-up towered over the 3D puzzle like a pilot's bridge on top of a boat. He had even attached a ladder so he'd be able to go up and use it. I hoped we wouldn't be driving under any low bridges.

"It looks like a Dr. Seuss car," said Molly.

"Look at the dents," Mom said, which made me wonder if she'd been to the carport even once since the Garbage Storms inflicted those dents. "You'd swear it was hit by thousands of marbles."

Dad was still thinking about the night before. "I'm very sorry for waking everyone and terrifying Kylie."

"It was no big deal," she assured him.

"And you already apologized," Molly said. "Twice."

"I needed to get some things from the front room. I wasn't thinking she might not have seen a flashlight for months."

Or a strange bear-like man trying to move a ham radio and its battery packs in the dark, I thought.

"It's okay, Mr. Weaver. Really."

Kylie showed just how over it she was by walking to the Fleetwood and claiming her spot inside, backseat, right. Mom, Molly, and I just watched, waiting for Dad's instructions.

"Good thing you didn't want a window," Molly whispered in my direction.

"Maybe she gets carsick," I said.

Dad stepped out of the carport to re-recheck the rope, bungee cords, and black Radio Shack electrical tape that held his creation together. He tapped the metal door on Nolab's Sky Kennel, which he'd fitted in next to the ham set. Not that Nolab was going to ride up there. The hard, gray plastic crate was crammed full of battery-starved electronics that once seemed like necessities. I made out two iPhones, Mom's Kindle, a control for my old X-box. Dad pointed out he could have packed even more stuff by stacking it on the trunk lid. But the trunk held supplies we would need on the road. We had to be able to open it. So the tailfins still rose like two metal mountains, separated by an unpopulated valley that was broad, smooth, and flat.

"I have a surprise, kids."

"Surprise?" Molly squealed.

He opened the trunk. "That day I went to Costco I was too late to find any canned goods. That's what I told you, and that was the truth... except for two boxes." He patted what had to be one of these boxes. "I'm sure someone hid them, planning to come back later. When we stop for lunch, we'll have pear halves and peaches. I've been saving them for a special occasion." Dad leaned back, giving himself space to close the trunk. "Getting out of our house will have to count." He moved closer to Mom, put his hand on her shoulder. She turned her head to kiss it. Molly smiled to see this, just as I did.

"Well," said Dad. "We'd better get going. The folks on the Ark are starting to wonder what's keeping us."

Taking hold of a silver door handle so that I could get in the car, I noticed that our refrigerator still displayed a magazine page Mom had taped to it in July as a joke. It was an ad from before the Drop Down. *Eat All You Want Without Gaining a Pound!* "One last thing, Adam." Feeling a hand on my shoulder, I turned to see Dad holding my camera. "You're in charge of documenting our trip."

Cradling it gently in my hands, I gazed at the Nikon D70 Mom found on Craigslist when I was starting seventh grade. She got it for me because photography had been the one other class I liked besides English. Since then, I had taken and stored more than 1,000 pictures.

Before I could remind Dad it still needed power, he handed me four AA batteries. "There are more if these go dead," he said.

After putting in the batteries, I walked to the end of our driveway and turned to take my first picture. *Life on Earth*, I imagined the title engraved on a small bronze nameplate. *Our House, 922 Palmetto Drive*. The photo was one of dozens displayed in the Adam Weaver Gallery, located on the main floor of NASA's Ark. Walking back to the Fleetwood, I felt a clutching in my gut, knowing that the place I had lived my entire life would soon be just a memory, joining almost everything else I once knew and took for granted.

Dad, Mom, Molly, and I squeezed into the car that wouldn't have required much squeezing a few months before. We backed out onto our street, turned, and drove quickly away. Our house disappeared in a blur of trees, gone like a page in a book slammed shut. A few minutes later, we pulled onto Interstate 75. The car pointed south, even though we could have gotten to Virginia faster by heading the other direction. Picking up Grammy meant taking the long way because driving to Newton took us toward Disney World and Universal Studios. After stopping for her,

Dad planned to drive past Orlando, then pick up I-95 North at Jacksonville.

He pulled his visor out sideways to shield him from the sun, which also hammered Molly. Brightness wasn't my problem. Stuck in the middle of the backseat with her on my left and Kylie on my right, I needed room: a place to stretch my arms; space to move my legs. Our house, it hit me now, had not been all that claustrophobic. The Cadillac Fleetwood, big as it was, seemed cramped, hot, and smelly. Having to wear our lumpy sand-lined jackets didn't help. Neither did Kylie's weights, two of which kept jabbing me.

This was no way to start an adventure.

But then I thought about other, more famous adventures like sailing from Europe to the so-called New World and rocketing to the moon. Those quests, it hit me now, had also been cramped and warm and stuffy.

Nothing's ever the way you picture it, which would be okay if it didn't mean everything always turned out worse than your expectations. Like Mom watching TV on election night. Or Dad in his store on Black Friday waiting for an onslaught of customers. Or me getting Seminole football gear as birthday presents from an aunt in Tallahassee who really didn't know me. "You'll find a lot of life is like that," Dad said my last birthday. "The presents look best while they're still wrapped."

I did have one question Christopher Columbus and the astronauts in Apollo 11 never had to deal with: Where was Grammy going to sit?

I scratched an itch on my cheek, which meant dislodging an arm from between me and Molly.

"Stop poking me." She scrunched up her nose like an angry pig.

"Real mature," I whispered. "Rated PG-3. For kids who act like they're three years old."

My sister looked even more ridiculous than usual that morning. Mom had sewn two big, bulging pockets on the front of her jacket, each about ten inches wide. These carried Bow Wow Dog and Mr. Beav, the stuffed animals deemed essential by Molly for sleeping at night. Bow Wow's face, made of bright orange fabric, looked out from the pocket with black button eyes like some freak kangaroo baby peeking at the world from its freak mother's pouch.

"Did you put on cologne, Adam?" she asked. "Because it doesn't make you stink any less, just different." Quickly, she added, "Ouch! Adam hit me!"

"Kids," Dad said in a deeper tone than usual, suggesting an imminent lecture. But that was all he said.

The breeze, at least, felt good. The windows were rolled down and Dad drove fast, his theory being it was best to race through pockets of Zero G, surprising the pockets before they surprised us. I focused on the camera, now resting on my lap, its strap pulled tightly around my arm. The car hit a dip; I held my breath. We didn't leave the ground. Looking up, I saw a lonely green highway sign. NEWTON 5.

"Five miles!" Molly shouted. "Five miles to where Grammy lives!"

"We can read," I said.

"Sorry," she snapped. "I keep forgetting we don't all have your massive brain."

Dad sneezed, the first of eight times. "Bless you," said Mom, the first three.

"It's hard to believe there's still pollen," he grumbled, before pinching his nose to block a final explosion. "But you know me. I've always loved nature. It's just that I'm allergic to it."

Every so often, we passed abandoned cars. Many were like ours, piled high with makeshift weights of every possible variety from jet skis to drum kits to bright red Coke machines like they'd been dumped on by a garage sale. Exiting for Newton, we saw a dead Golden Retriever floating four feet off the ground, tethered to its own chain. Probably stiff as a rock, his tail pointed straight up, as did his ears. Poor guy. Before choking on his collar, he'd likely been one of those dogs who ran out their lives in circles, a hard metal post at the center of their existence. I wished he had lived on our street. I would have freed him like I had the Dalmatian in the yard kitty-corner from ours right after the Garbage Storms. Even if the Golden Retriever had floated away after a while, just like the Dalmatian must have done, it wouldn't have been without knowing what freedom felt like.

Minutes later, we pulled into Newton Quality Care. The place looked stranger than usual, and it didn't take long to figure out why. Except for our car, the parking lot was empty.

"We don't all have to go in," Dad said while taking a spot marked Emergency Vehicles Only in front of the main entrance.

"I want to find Grammy," Molly declared.

"I want to know if my grandpa's alive," Kylie said.

A silver spray can peeked out from under the seat. I pushed it back with my foot, hoping to hide it. I think Kylie saw me.

I felt lightheaded as I got out of the car, and it hit me this was the first place outside of our home we'd been to in months. As I remembered from visiting Grammy before, the building took the shape of a big X with four long corridors sticking out from a central point. The windows were small and dark and reflected the skinny palm trees that bordered the lot. Their fronds curving upward, the trees looked like gray-green umbrellas turned inside out by strong wind.

When I took my photo, I zoomed in on a window, choosing the framed reflection instead of the real trees behind me.

CHAPTER FOURTEEN

Fountain of Youth... Just Add Wa-

WELCOME TO NEWTON QUALITY CARE, greeted the sign on the building's brick wall. But the warmth of these words, blue and bold against a background of white, were quickly chilled by the graffiti that followed: *WHERE TIME HAS ALWAYS BEEN RUNNING OUT.*

Kylie surprised us by walking back across the lot toward the palm trees. Stopping near the lot's far side, she turned to face us, her eyes fixed on me. Was she waiting for me to join her? There was only one way to find out, and sure enough, when I got close, she quietly asked, "What's with the spray can you're hiding?" Dad and Molly were watching, Dad with a look that clearly said, *Whatever's going on here, please make it quick.* Mom was walking Nolab. She looked over too, once the dog found a shrub worth peeing on.

"It's nothing."

"If it was nothing," Kylie continued, "then how was I able to see it?"

In a hushed voice, I said, "Wire Detangler."

"Wire Detangler?" Kylie asked.

"It was one of Radio Shack's big sellers."

"Radio Shack had big sellers?"

I told her the story. It started when I was nine. Dad called a family meeting. He told me and Mom he planned to patent his "once-in-a-lifetime invention." After dumping out a grocery bag of ear buds with their cords all twisted up, he said, "If you put two wires within a foot of each other they get tangled." He held up a plain-silver spray can. "Wire Detangler undoes the mess." He let loose with it.

If Mom was impressed, she didn't show it. "I want to be supportive," she said, "but look how greasy it got everything." She wasn't so sure it was worth spending five-thousand dollars to get a patent. "I'll think about it," she told him, but I don't think she ever did, at least not in a positive way.

Dad didn't give up. Thinking his superiors at Radio Shack might want to be part of the next Earth-changing innovation, he repeated the presentation at their West Florida office. They took Mom's side. Wire Detangler was messy, not to mention useless. Not the kind of thing they wanted their name on. When Dad got home that night, he poured himself a tall bronze-colored drink and tossed his invention in the trash.

"My violin teacher had a plaque on her wall," Kylie interjected. "With a quote from some saint. *He who makes no mistakes makes nothing.*"

"Dad's invention wasn't a mistake. Like I told you, it was a big seller. But Dad never got any credit."

Her eyes widened.

"Wire D-Tangler. 'Because you can't put two wires within a foot of each other without them getting tangled.' Same words. It had to be someone Dad showed it to."

Kylie never asked why I pulled Dad's spray can out of the trash, and I never told her what I was thinking when I did: how I was going to make things right, how the world was going to know.

She glanced over at my family. "That's sad."

"Yes," I said. "That's Dad."

Kylie started walking back across the parking lot. I was right behind. "It really costs five-thousand dollars to get a patent?" she asked.

"Twice that sometimes. For lawyers and stuff."

Mom was putting Nolab back in the car. "Did you propose to her, Adam?" Molly called out, just loud enough for anyone within a two-mile radius to hear. I wanted to propose swapping Molly for Grammy to save space on the trip.

"Well," Dad said as he pulled open the entrance door.

The hair on my arms tingled when I saw how dark it was inside. But it got worse, scary worse, the instant Dad turned on his flashlight. Molly screamed. There was a body on the ceiling. Dad quickly aimed the flashlight lower, straight down the long corridor, but we had all seen the bone-thin corpse floating just below the ceiling like some strange inflatable toy.

The stench argued even louder than the body for "Get out of here! Turn around!" Newton Quality Care had always smelled bad, like a restroom with a dirty changing table. But now... I looked over at Kylie, trying to make myself focus on something besides the potential for puking.

We saw the gray shape of another corpse close to the ceiling. "Do you think they just died naturally, from something besides Zero G?" Mom half whispered, like the dead were going to hear us. "Otherwise, why not just push yourself down from the ceiling?"

"Grammy!" I shouted. "Where are you?"

"Grammy!" Molly shouted too. "Tell us you're not dead like the people on the ceiling!"

Without Dad's flashlight, the corridor would have been totally dark. Though the building had lots of windows, they didn't seem to open onto the hallways. My eyes were adjusting to the dim light, and it was hard not to glance at the bodies. None had been young enough to be nurses or attendants, making me think the workers had simply abandoned the place, leaving the patients alone.

We reached the stone sculpture that used to be a fountain.

Water no longer spilled from the outstretched palm of Juan Ponce de Leon, the explorer who looked for the fountain of youth – which made placing this fountain in the middle of an assisted-living facility more than borderline cruel, since it never worked any better at making people young again than the ones Ponce came across in real life. It was like letting history's worst explorer taunt everyone who passed: "You won't find it either."

"The crossroads," Mom said. "Where the corridors meet. If we keep going straight, we'll find Grammy's room."

"I'll be right back," Kylie said quietly before disappearing into the darkness on our right.

"I've got a second flashlight in the car," Dad called after her.

"I think she's had enough of your flashlights," Mom said.

"Adam?" A quiet voice floated our way from far down the hall. "Molly?"

Grammy appeared in the distance, ghostlike in the grayness.

"Grammy!?!" Molly and I shouted together.

She looked thin, something Grammy had never been, not even in photos from the Middle Ages when Dad was a baby. Not that she looked emaciated or skeletal like the bodies on the ceiling. More like what skinny people used to call "normal," back when they ran the world. Slowly she came toward us, using a stout metal filing cabinet as walker. A white wrap that could have been a nightgown flapped around her as she moved.

"Molly!" she shouted. "You've lost weight!"

"That's Kylie," said Molly – and sure enough, Kylie was back. "She watched her parents die," Molly added. "She didn't seem too shook up about it."

Kylie looked surprised and hurt. When she noticed me watching, she turned her face away.

"That's a real shame," Grammy said, giving no hint about which part of Molly's announcement bothered her. Then, looking up at one of the bodies on the ceiling, she snarled, "Oh, hey. Good morning, Crabapple Peggy. You're not looking so well. Meanness get the better of you?"

She may have lost weight, but Grammy had lost none of what made her Grammy. As feisty as she was funny, she always got me laughing with the weird stuff she said. Like if you asked her how old she was, she'd reply, "Why don't you ask me something interesting, like what color were the dinosaurs I saw from my school bus?"

If anyone had asked me, Grammy never belonged in this place, going back to when Grandpa was alive and needed extra care. She just never seemed old or helpless. Not even after she started showing what Mom called her "memory problems" and Dad called "her creative past." It was her choice to stay after Grandpa died. No one had pushed her.

"Where's my Bill?" she asked now. "I've been looking all over."

Placing his hand on her shoulder, Dad said, "You know Bill's no longer with us."

I hadn't noticed at first, but Kylie now possessed a second walkie-talkie. She held the new one in her hand. "My grandpa," she said without emotion. "He's dead."

"Oh, sweetie," Mom said. "That's awful."

"A real shame," Grammy added. "But maybe we should finish catching up outside. You did bring a car, of course?"

"You okay?" I asked Kylie.

She just shrugged.

Mom asked Grammy, "Are you the only one here? How did you make it this long?"

"It was hard," Grammy said, while pushing her filing cabinet walker a foot in the direction of the main entrance. "Hardest thing I've been through. Got to see our dark sides. Real dog-eat-dog."

Molly gasped. "Dogs eat other dogs?"

"It's just a figure of speech, Pumpkin," Dad said.

"What *did* you eat?" Mom asked.

"Beans, flour, cornmeal… whatever I could find." Grammy looked around uneasily, like a mouse checking for cats, which made me wonder just how alone we were. "Not everyone here was so lucky. Or determined. Some just didn't want to keep going."

"Giving up," Dad said, his voice barely a whisper, "I still don't understand it."

"If you'd been here, you might." Grammy was looking around again. "But most held on long as they could."

"We're on our way to NASA's Ark," Dad said. "We can head out—"

"Count me in," Grammy said.

"As soon as you're ready."

"That would be six months ago." She looked around again, peering hard into the dark corridors. "I've had it with this stink hole. We need to get moving."

"Well." Dad scratched his middle chin. "Who wants to ride on the trunk lid? We've got extra rope, and I won't drive so fast."

I saw this question for what it was: my first chance to play hero for Kylie. She sure wasn't volunteering.

"I'll do it," I said.

"Grammy's teeny," Molly protested, staring at Kylie. "Any one of us could give up *her* place for Grammy who's really part of this family."

When Kylie said nothing, I assured the others, "I'll be okay. I'm not scared of riding outside."

Seeing the walkie-talkies, Grammy asked Kylie, "Where'd you find those useless toys? I tried using one, couldn't get the crud-piece to work. I talked and talked, but it might as well been a seashell. 'Cept I couldn't hear the sea."

"Maybe you kept holding the talk button down," Kylie said.

"Because I heard you, and told them. That's why we're here."

"You kids and your gadgets," Grammy said. "You should've been here to help me."

"Hey, y'all!" A shout out of the blackness.

Molly screamed. The rest of us jumped.

"Mrs. Weaver?" Some guy a few years older than me appeared in the glare of Dad's flashlight. "It's just me! Baker! Don't shoot!"

"We'd need a gun for that," Molly said, causing Dad to aim the flashlight at her face. This was a sensitive topic for him, the most sensitive possible. Dad had his reasons for hating guns.

Baker came closer. "Mrs. Weaver? Is this your family?" On top of having blond Ken-doll hair, he looked muscular, athletic. His eyes were doll-like too, an artificially perfect blue. Like Kylie, he had wrapped himself in stuff: a small flat-screen TV; two laptops; and yes, cast-iron weightlifting plates. "Hey!" he said, pointing at Kylie and her weights. "Great minds, you know, they do things together."

First impression confirmed: pretty as a Ken doll and almost as smart.

"You nearly gave us heart attacks," Dad said. "Who are you?"

"Baker," Grammy said. "Helped me survive." She sounded nervous, especially for Grammy who never seemed rattled by anything. "Helped the others too." Her voice faded to a whisper. "Whether or not they asked."

"I know this sounds weird," Kylie said, "but didn't you play for Newton?"

Smiling, Baker nodded. Which surprised me since he looked too old to have played against our middle school team. All I could think was he'd flunked a few years.

"I knew it! I knew it! You tackled my boyfriend Q. He's dead now."

"I never tackled anyone that hard." Baker didn't sound like he was joking. "Mrs. Weaver here's a great lady," he said next.

"She told me she might have kin showing up. She told me y'all would get her out. I figured I had to help her." He then asked Dad, "Do you really have room in your car for all of us?"

"Baker can sit on the trunk," Kylie said. "With me."

CHAPTER FIFTEEN

Road Rage

We were barely out of the parking lot when Grammy said, "We gotta ditch that Baker monster." She was squeezed in tight between Molly and me. "Only reason he kept me alive is he thought I'd be his ticket out. Guess he was right to think that."

"He kept you alive?" Dad said. "How?"

"By not killing me like the others."

"A serial killer," Molly said. "No wonder Kylie likes him."

"Floor it!" Grammy commanded. "Hard right! Now! Throw off that sick parasite!"

Dad didn't floor it or take a hard right. "Not a great idea," he said instead. "And even if it was, I tied those ropes well."

"He killed my Bill," Grammy added, which made me question everything she just told us. My grandfather had passed away long before the Drop Down.

"Now, Mom," Dad said. "You know he's been gone for years."

"He did it to get our food. So he could stay alive. Wasn't even smart enough to take the bodies outside. Or maybe just plum lazy."

I looked out the back windshield. Saying stuff I couldn't hear, Baker slid a few inches closer to Kylie who didn't slide away like she should have. I caught myself wishing something I hadn't wished since school, what I used to wish whenever I passed girls like Kylie Cho in the hall. I wished I was special. Or at least less un-special.

Grammy was still talking. "There's got to be a way to lose him once and for all."

"Besides," Dad said. "Your Mr. Baker is sitting on the trunk lid of a moving car. That hardly makes him a danger to us, even if what you're saying is true."

"If what I'm saying is true? Did I just hear my son correctly?"

"We'll sort this out—"

Whatever else Dad planned to say, it got preempted by a powerful thud. Mom screamed as the windshield in front of her turned dark and gooey. "Oh dear God, what is that?"

"Some monster bug," Molly said. "Like in a movie I saw on TV."

"I think it's an armadillo," Dad calmly noted. "See? Don't those look like pieces of shell?"

"Whatever it was," Mom said, "it's sure disgusting now."

"We must have gone through a patch of Zero G," Dad said. "He must have been floating in our path."

Following the armadillo's example, our conversation died. Mom was no longer the only one staring out a window wishing she were somewhere else.

Dad drove slower now that we had riders on the trunk. The dial on the speedometer pointed at 40. We passed an old army tank painted in sandy desert colors. "Now there's a great set of wheels," Dad said. "For traveling in Low G, at least."

"And no one's going to mess with him," Molly said.

We went back to not talking.

Minutes later, a huge orange truck shot past us. "Snow plow," said Grammy. "Probably not from these parts."

"I wonder where they're heading," Dad said. "If they're coming out of Tampa, the best way to the Ark was I-75. A lot more direct to Virginia."

"I need a rest area," Molly declared, which was just what I'd been thinking.

"We don't need a rest area," Dad said. "We can stop anywhere.

It's not like there's anyone around to see us."

"These fields are lovely," Mom said, her sarcasm thick as windshield goo. "I especially like the comfort and privacy they provide."

"Excuse me," Dad said, matching her tone, "but I thought some fresh air might be good. And it's not like we're going to find toilets that flush."

"I'll settle for walls," she said.

As if on cue, a distant blue sign announced, REST AREA 1 MILE.

"Well," said Dad, "rest area it is." Turning to Mom, he asked, "You want to drive afterward? I'm pretty sleepy."

"I'm not all that awake myself," she replied. "What if Adam tried taking the wheel?" As ideas went, this didn't sound that crazy. Dad had given me an early driving lesson one Sunday in May in the parking lot outside Molly's school. And even if it took place in a Honda Civic half the size of this car, the steering wheel and pedals had all been in the same places. "I don't think he's going to run into anyone," Mom continued. "I can help him get started."

I must have smiled, because Dad said, "I wouldn't get too excited, Adam. Driving 40 miles an hour is not as much fun as it looks."

Two minutes later, we reached our stop, pulling in next to a yellow bulldozer that took up two Handicapped spots. Its blade rested a foot off the pavement and its thick metal track came up to the bottom of our windows. "Hello!" Dad shouted as we rolled out of the Fleetwood. "Anyone here?" Receiving no answer, he shook his head. "Looks like the end of the line for this one."

The beige brick building stank, even from the curb some thirty feet away. I waited for Dad to ask Mom, "How's that pretty green field looking to you now?" and was glad when he didn't.

Baker had already unfastened his and Kylie's rope. "I'll guard the car," he volunteered. "I don't need no bathroom. I thought maybe Mrs. Weaver and I could have a moment."

"You gotta be kidding," Grammy exploded. "I'm 74 years old and I've been sitting in a car for an hour."

"Hey, hey, not a problem," Baker said with a fake laugh. "You go on in and pee. Just don't be making up stories. Your family's good people, I can see that. They don't need no tales." He turned to Dad, and whispered, "Memory problems. Can't trust a thing she says."

"I hadn't noticed," said Dad.

"It's serious alright," Baker said. "Believe me. Y'all didn't hear stories from her in the car?"

"The only thing they heard from me," Grammy said gruffly, "was how much old people like me miss songbirds. Some of us think God flung off the wrong noise makers."

"So what were you?" Dad asked Baker. "A nurse's aide? The janitor?"

"He didn't work at Newton," Grammy said. "He lived nearby. After his parents floated off, he came sniffing for food."

"Sounds familiar," said Molly.

"I did too work for Newton," Baker said. "See what I mean? Memory problems."

Grammy shook her head. Moving toward the rest area doors, she muttered, "I wish I had memory problems. Then I could blot you out of my mind."

"I'm still going to watch the car," Baker said as Molly and Mom started toward the building. "We don't know the story with this bulldozer. Could be a trap."

"I'll stay too," said Dad, who probably felt a serious need to guard his car from its guard. "Perhaps Baker will help me scrape the armadillo off our windshield."

Starting to walk away, I heard Baker say, "Like, uh, Kylie said something about getting on an Ark. That goes with what Mrs. Weaver told me, back at the place." I slowed my pace so I could eavesdrop. "She said her son was one smart dude, that he'd have something up his sleeve."

"Well, I don't know about that. But I do have some plans for getting us through this."

Dad, I wanted to shout, *reactivate your smarm detector. Grammy knows this guy and doesn't trust him.*

"You need me along," Baker went on. "I can help when things get tough. With crowds and stuff, all those sickos and psychos straggling about. I used to be one badass football player. It takes a lot to rattle me."

Like Grammy, I shook my head as I walked to the building.

A girl pointed a gun at us, turning the bones in my legs to foam rubber. She and a boy were huddled on the tile floor, pressed together as one, right below the empty racks that once offered free Florida roadmaps and flyers for alligator farms.

"Gun!" Molly shouted, while Mom reached out to pull her close. I tried to say something, but nothing came out. I was also distracted by Kylie who must not have heard Molly. Coming in a different set of glass doors than the ones we had used, she walked straight into the Women's room.

"Don't come," the girl stammered, "close." She looked a few years younger than me, while the boy was maybe six. They were both big like us. The gun was big, too. It shook in her hand.

"Who are you?" she demanded, her voice a bit less shaky. "You don't look like Skulls."

"Skulls?" said Grammy.

This left it to me to share the marauders' stupid name. "Skullectors," I said. "They call themselves Skullectors." In a good sci-fi novel they would have been Skull Frackers or Bangers or Pluckers. "They dress and act like pirates," I added. "They fly the Jolly Roger."

Mom stared at me like I was making things up. "Dad knows," I said quietly. "We heard about them on his ham."

"Your father knew about this?" Mom said in a tone that had me worried for Dad.

"Mom, Adam," Molly sputtered. "The gun?"

The girl and boy stared back at us through huge blue eyes, wide and round, like you might see in a bad painting. Hanging on a wall in somebody's guestroom, it could have looked cute. Here, it just made them look frightened.

"They got our mom," said the girl.

"Mama's gone," added her brother. "Keys, too. Mama wouldn't give them up."

"Those aren't so important now," said the girl. "Not since the prisoners stole our extra fuel."

"Prisoners?" asked Mom.

"You know," the girl replied, "convicts."

Mom took a few steps back, pushed open a glass door, and called for Dad to come inside. "Now!"

He came running in, leaving Baker with the car.

"I thought the prisons were all locked down," Mom said. "Permanently, now that the power's out. Isn't that what you told me?"

Dad didn't seem to hear her.

"Put the gun down," he said, taking one step toward the girl on the floor. "We're not going to harm you."

"We just don't want trouble," the girl said.

"You're holding the trouble in your hand. Gently now, on the floor."

Baker, who must have snuck in behind Dad, chose that instant to charge at the girl. He snarled like a dog with rabies.

She screamed as her gun hit the floor and slid a few inches.

Still growling, Baker pinned her to the floor. You could hear the crack when her head hit the tiles.

"Good Lord," said Grammy, as Dad and I jumped forward.

I grabbed his right shoulder while Dad seized the other. Together we pulled him back off of the girl.

"Let's everyone take a breath," Dad said.

I looked around, but still no Kylie, which irritated me. Not because she'd missed the way I'd bravely grabbed Baker, though that wouldn't have hurt. I wished she had witnessed his brutality.

The girl sat up, and rubbing the back of her head, started crying like a six year old. You could say she cried exactly like a six year old, because it was hard to tell where her cries ended and her brother's began.

Mom knelt beside the girl and gently placed her arms around her.

"Where were you headed?" Dad asked.

She managed to stop crying. "Magnet City."

"Magnet City?"

"Where the Magnet People live."

Our confusion must have shown.

"They wear magnets on their feet and clothes," she said. "To keep from floating off. It's right outside Disney World."

"What do the magnets hold onto?" I asked, but the boy had cheered up, and was squealing. "Disney World! Disney World!"

"Our Uncle Matthias is there," the girl said.

Mom looked up at Dad. "Who are these Skullectors? Where do they come from?"

Dad cleared his throat and looked away. "Brevard Correctional," he said quietly. "Someone there forgot to flip the Closed for Business switch."

"Brevard?" Mom said.

"Near Cape Canaveral."

"They visited us, too," Grammy said. "Blackbeard. That's

89

what they call their leader."

"You met Blackbeard?" Dad asked quietly.

Nolab rubbed against my leg. Someone (Baker) had left a car door open, and the dog had followed him inside.

"He's traveling to other jails," Grammy said, "trying to build a convict army. That's what he told us. But those prisons were all locked down. There was no busting them open."

"I haven't heard about them for weeks," Dad said. "I figured the Skulls were done pillaging. That there wasn't much left to steal."

"They wanted our keys," said the girl. "But Mama wouldn't give them up. She was still holding them when she fell into the sky."

"They wanted our food," Grammy said. "But we scared them off. Told them we had some contagious disease."

Mom was still glaring at Dad. "What else have you been keeping from us?"

"Blackbeard. His real name's Travis Funnell."

"Travis Funnell?" I said. "The Lunch Money Thief?" I'd heard about him at school, the accountant who stole from the Florida Online Lunch Pay Program. He was the reason they stopped serving lunch back when I was in sixth grade.

"One and the same," Dad said. "Public Enemy Number One. Star of TV News. He stopped shaving in prison, and started calling himself Blackbeard. He wears a bandana."

"Does he have a parrot?" Molly asked.

Dad actually smiled as he said, "None of this matters. We're not going to run into him."

"We know he's on this highway," Mom said.

"There are other ways to get across Florida." He looked at the kids on the rest area floor. "And to Magnet City."

The girl seemed puzzled.

"That's right," said Dad. "It's on our way." He scratched his middle chin, a few beats longer than usual. "You two can ride on the trunk," he said at last. "If you're okay with that. There's room for two more. If anything, the weight will help."

Dad, it seemed, was done talking about Blackbeard and the Skulls. Good thing too, since Molly and Mom didn't need to know how the Skullectors got their name. They were cannibals who kept souvenirs.

"Do you have names?" Molly asked the newly orphaned sister and brother.

"I'm Jade," answered the girl. "He's Jude."

"I'll take the gun," Baker said. "We don't need anyone else getting the better of us."

"Just leave it," Dad said. "What we don't need is the danger." But this came too late. Baker examined his new prize, pointing it straight up toward the ceiling.

"What did I miss?" asked Kylie, coming out of the Women's room.

CHAPTER SIXTEEN

Driver's Seat

Dad handed me the keys.

Baker said, "I'd like to drive."

"But Dad said—" I stopped when I saw the thin smile on his face and how he was holding the gun. He was rubbing the barrel like he expected a genie to pop out of it.

"Listen, Baker," Dad said.

"It's okay," I said. "He wants to go the same place we're going."

Dad's eyes narrowed, but in the end he shrugged. "Just put that stupid gun away." He walked over to Mom who couldn't have looked more worried, and put his hand on her shoulder.

"You're really letting him drive?" she asked.

"I'm tired," he said. "We all are. So long as he knows east from west, we'll be okay." He looked back at Baker. "But take it easy. We'll still have riders on the trunk."

Those riders turned out to be Molly and me, squished in behind Jade and Jude. The trunk lid was crowded. Dad's ropes pinched and burned.

It wasn't like getting to drive.

"I see your girlfriend's riding up front now," said Molly.

"She's not my girlfriend. You don't know anything."

Twisting around as far as I could, I watched Dad, in the back behind Kylie, looking at an Atlas. I knew what he was doing: preparing a back-roads route to Magnet City to avoid the Skulls. He confirmed this by telling Baker to take the next exit.

When Dad nodded off a few minutes later, the Atlas slid off

his lap and Baker hit the gas. I was thrown against the ropes. Molly shrieked. Jude started bawling. I looked through the window to see Mom leaning forward, shouting at Baker.

The car slowed down, though not to a speed Dad would have approved. The ropes burned with every bump. I held tight to my camera.

The breeze whipped Molly's hair into her face. "You should've grabbed that gun." She covered her face with her hands. "Murderers make sucky drivers."

"So," I asked Jade and Jude, "where's home?"

"Fort Myers," Jade replied. "Our uncle told Mama to take us to Magnet City right after the Garbage Storms. She wasn't convinced. Then, two weeks ago, Grandpa died. That's where we were living."

Baker hit a dip, and bouncing back out, the car left the ground. We must have been airborne a good twelve feet, or as measured in the time we all stopped breathing: one-thousand-one, one-thousand-two, one-thousand-three. The landing felt surprisingly gentle, not like in a movie chase where sparks shoot out and hubcaps fly off. The Low G had cushioned us.

"I'm hungry," Jude muttered.

"You should have said something before we left," his sister said.

Twisting my body to look back inside the car, I saw Dad twitching. Probably having bad dreams, which was hardly surprising given the way our whole adventure had turned into one. Nolab, on Dad's lap, was twitching too.

Molly leaned closer to me. Her dancing hair slapped my face. "Are you scared?"

I was. And with Baker holding both steering wheel and gun, I was more afraid by the minute. But I couldn't tell my sister that.

"We'll be fine." I put my hand on hers. "Who would have thought we'd make it this far? Dad's plan to get on the Ark might be nine-tenths crazy, but stranger things have happened."

"Like when he hit a baseball into space?"

"Like when he hit that baseball into space."

Molly was smiling. I was too. In our minds, we were reliving one of the few good memories the Drop Down had given us. A full two months after the first, famous baseball shot up into the stratosphere from the game Dad took me to, Molly and I stood in our backyard. It was late June, and late in the evening. Our eyes were on Dad who held his old bat, ready to hit a ball. With one solid crack, that ball soared up and out of sight, becoming one with the gray-blue sky. It might have been the biggest we ever saw him smile.

"Out of the park," Molly said, using the same words Dad shouted that night.

Maybe an hour later, the Fleetwood slowed and pulled off to the side. An orange grove backed up to the narrow sandy shoulder. I wanted to stand and move my legs. I also wanted some lunch.

Jade and I got our ropes untied fast, then helped our siblings off the trunk.

I opened the front passenger door for Kylie. "Thanks," she said without looking at me.

Dad still slept in the backseat. He didn't budge when I lifted Nolab off his lap.

"So what's he got against guns anyway?" Baker asked Mom and Grammy.

"Plenty," said Grammy. "My Bill used to keep one. For protection, he said."

Baker nodded. "Why sure."

"Because of that gun," Grammy continued, "my boy here grew up without an older brother."

"You ain't saying?"

"Chet was ten years older. First summer he was home from

college, he came in late one night. My Bill's first thought at two in the morning wasn't *college kid behaving like a college kid*, but *home invader*. He snuck into the kitchen and shot his own boy."

"He killed his son?"

"Didn't say that. Chet was lucky his old man couldn't shoot for squat. Got off with a minor leg wound."

"Through and through?" Baker asked excitedly. "Or just grazed?"

"Neither. My Bill winged him in his Walkman. That's a CD player… you probably don't remember those. Shattered it, blasting fragments from some thrash-metal CD into Chet's leg. Never got all the Shrapnel out."

"He still had shrapnel in his leg?" Kylie asked.

"Times two," Grammy said with a smile. "That was the name of the band. Shrapnel."

"Hardly life threatening," Baker noted.

"Our Chet was never too good at that forgiveness thing. He got so ticked that, when he left the E.R., he limped right out of our lives. Hardly came home anymore, except when his laundry piled up or cash ran out. Once college was done, moved flat straight to California. Needed to escape the humidity, he said. But I knew better."

"So Mr. Weaver grew up hating guns?" Baker said.

Mom shrugged. "He never cared much for heavy metal music either."

"Think we should get him up?" Grammy asked. But before anyone answered, Dad jerked awake.

"Well!" he exclaimed. "I just had the worst rising nightmare."

"I get them too," Baker said. "In place of the falling ones I used to have."

"We all get them, Einstein," Molly said just loud enough for me to hear.

"An orchard?" Dad said. "Didn't we just stop?"

"Lunch," Kylie said. "Someone promised us peaches and pears."

"Though I do need to find a private spot," Mom said.

"Like Mr. Weaver said, didn't we just stop for a bathroom break?" Kylie asked.

"The rest of us didn't have the same relaxing experience you did," Grammy said. She started for the trees, with Mom and Molly doing the same, but taking different paths. Kylie stayed behind, talking with Baker. I helped Dad get food out of the trunk while Jade and Jude squeezed in to watch. After that, I set off on my own trail into the orchard. "Hey, Jude," I heard Jade say behind me, "show a little patience. You're not the only one starving here."

The sonic boom of a gunshot tore the tranquil scene in half. A second blast followed. I ran back toward the car, sure Baker had shot Dad.

Dad was okay, but not very happy looking.

Baker was grinning.

"I've about had it with you and your gun," Dad said.

"Target practice," Baker said calmly. "I ain't fired one of these since before the Drop Down. I needed to make sure it worked the same. For when I need it."

"Right," Dad said, not hiding his sarcasm.

"Look at them oranges," Baker went on, pointing into the grove. "I aimed straight. It shot straight. Low G didn't affect it one tad."

"Help!" Mom cried from deep in the grove – straight in the direction Baker was pointing.

CHAPTER SEVENTEEN

By the Seat of My Pants

"Help!" Mom called again. "Hurry!"

I ran as fast as I could. Dad was close behind.

"Adam!"

I looked up and saw her. She was twenty feet in the air, clinging to a branch, upside down, her shoes pointing up toward the sky.

I didn't see blood; she hadn't been shot.

"Stop!" she shouted. "Zero G right there!"

"Listen to your mother," Dad said. He stood next to me with Molly behind him.

"Mom!" Molly pushed forward, but Dad pulled her back.

"Slow down, Pumpkin," he cautioned. "We can't simply jump up and pull Mom back down. We need to think this through."

"I've got it," I said. "Mom needs to get to the next higher branch. It almost touches this tree. We climb up this one and pull her over."

"I was never very good at climbing," Molly said.

"Me neither," I admitted. "But I'm betting that's changed. Help me get started."

"You bet," Dad said, stepping forward to give me a lift with his hands. "Just hold on tight and be careful."

For the most part, my hunch about climbing proved right. I moved like I was six years old, nimble and light. But my size made it difficult to fit where I needed to fit. Twigs scraped and poked all over my body. I heard lots of snapping.

Then I got stuck. The tree had gripped my sweatpants in at least two separate places. I tried to shift sideways but couldn't. I tried lowering myself – still stuck. I reached down with my hands, but couldn't bend my body forward enough to help them locate the problem. I even tried pushing myself away from the tree, thinking I'd break loose, either rising or falling, while getting the chance to grab a new branch. The tree wouldn't let go.

"Dad?"

"It's okay, Adam. There's one thing you can do."

"Like?"

"Leave your pants."

Looking down and around, I saw only Dad and Molly.

"She's not here to watch," said Molly.

"That's not what I was thinking," I lied. "I don't care if Kylie sees me." Not that her being there would have stopped me. It just would have made it harder.

"There are extra clothes in the trunk," Dad said. "You'll have pants once we're back at the car."

"Okay," I said, "here goes nothing," which unfortunately proved true. I squirmed and tugged with all my strength, yet only moved two inches at most.

"It's not working," I called.

Suddenly, I felt movement, not from me, but the pants. The waistband was sliding down my skin, slowly but steadily. "I've got them," said Dad from a few branches below.

The biggest struggle came with getting my shoes through the legs. We did this one foot at a time, one fraction of an inch at a time.

"Thanks," I said, climbing again. The branches poked and scratched worse than before. But I didn't care; it felt good to be moving.

Once I was level with Mom's upside down face, I faced a bigger challenge. She wouldn't let go. "Come on, Mom," I coaxed. "We're closer than I thought we'd be. You don't need to move any higher up the tree. Just push yourself this way. I'll grab hold of your hand."

"I can't, honey. I'm sorry. My fingers just won't move."

"I'm climbing up to the next branches," I said. "They almost touch your tree. When you let go, your hand will come straight to mine."

"They look pretty thin," Dad called from below, but I was already moving. "Adam, be careful." My heart pounded. My senses seemed magnified. The orange smell went straight to my brain, like someone was spraying air freshener close to my face. My palms felt tender where they pressed against the bark.

I heard Molly say, "It's not going to work."

"Thanks for your support," I muttered, "though I'll settle for the tree's." I kept climbing.

"Look, Mom, almost there." Breathing like a runner who just finished a marathon, I found a solid limb. "One more time. You've got to let go. I'll be able to reach you."

She seemed to cling even harder. I saw terror in her eyes, but this gave me hope. The same mom who had talked about going to the beach and giving up did not want to die. "Come on, Mom," I said quietly as two tiny, white mealy bugs crawled onto the back of my hand. "Trust me."

I tried to move closer, felt my own branch grow thin. From back near the trunk, I heard the sound of cracking. Gravity – just when I didn't need it. I held tight to the limb overhead.

"Do it, Mom!" Molly shouted. "Or I'll walk into the Zero G!"

"We need you, Mom," I added quietly while flicking my wrist and watching two tiny white dots take a sharp upward turn. Zero G, as close as my hand.

Looking down at her daughter, Mom let go with one hand.

"Now, Mom! Now!" Molly shouted as three puny oranges popped off her tree, falling straight up.

"Okay," Mom said, releasing her hold. "I'm all yours."

I stretched out and grabbed her hand.

"Great, Mom, great! We're going to be all right!" I pulled her over to my tree, and her body dropped slowly until she was right side up. My hand hurt from the way she gripped it.

Climbing back down, coaxing Mom the whole way, I felt Dad holding my legs, his hands like hard metal shackles that nothing could break. Finally, Mom was on the ground, flat on her back, her breath as loud as breaking waves, her face as pale as sugar sand. The rest of us leaned in over her.

"Thank you, Adam," she whispered. "And Molly." She looked at Dad. My heart was pounding.

"Well done, son," he said, patting me on the shoulder. He, too, had shed his pants, revealing legs as white as the belly of a fish.

"Dad?"

"Go ahead, Adam. Take mine." He held them out between us. "I'll dress at the car."

"You can wait for me there," Mom said. "All of you. I still need that break, now more than ever. Don't worry. I'll be careful."

"Are you sure?" Dad said.

"When I walk back, I'll grab some leaves or twigs, and toss them out in front of me."

"Why?" said Molly.

"To see if they rise."

Molly stayed with her, refusing to budge.

When Dad and I reached the car, Jade handed me a can of pears. Her brother clutched a bag of Cheese Puffs. Every few seconds, Jude released one to the air, catching it with his mouth as it rose.

Coming around from the back of the car, Dad smiled. He was wearing pants again.

"You're not eating," Jade said to me.

"Sorry." I plucked a pear half from the can.

"There are forks in the trunk," Dad said. "Big box of them."

Mom and Molly appeared, holding hands as they walked out from the trees. "Where's Nolab?" Molly asked.

"There," Jade said, pointing behind me.

I turned. Kylie was some fifty feet away, coming toward us. She had Nolab on a leash.

"We've been making friends," she called out while looking down at him. "Haven't we?"

Nolab growled, weakly this time.

"Go on, boy." Kylie let go of the leash. It fell ever so slowly to the ground. "Go to Adam," she commanded. "Go to Molly."

"No," I hollered. "Don't let him run loose. We already found one patch of Zero G."

Nolab lurched forward, picking up speed, such as it was, his wide frame rocking back and forth. Then just as I'd feared, he left the ground. I jumped forward, trying to catch his leash, but didn't come close, not with both Dad and Molly grabbing me.

Poor pup. The first few inches quickly became feet. Nolab paddled frantically with his front paws while his rear end and stubby spear of a tail tumbled upward and forward, turning in a slow-motion summersault. His leash chain, too, spun round and round, creating a kind of shimmering halo. I felt tears welling up, felt tightness in my throat.

It was Mom who charged forward and caught hold of the leash, yanking Nolab from flight like a fish hooked by a fisherman. Her speed got her through the pocket of Zero G. She fell to the ground between Kylie and Baker.

Molly erupted. "You tried to kill him on purpose! You knew he'd float away!"

Kylie seemed shaken. "But I never thought—"

Mom was climbing onto her feet. Nolab was back on the

ground, his charcoal-black eyes darting every which way.

"Did you see that fat thing lift off!?" Baker said, coming out of the grove. His grin made me want to hurl him into the Zero G. "That ain't no wiener dog! It's a Supersized Whopper dog!"

Dad stepped in front of me, keeping me in place. "Back in the car," he said, his voice forceful without getting loud. "Everyone."

Walking toward us, Kylie skirted the spot where Nolab took off. Mom and Baker walked just behind her. Every few steps, Mom had to tug at the leash, Nolab reluctant to lift off again.

"She knew that would happen," Molly said to me. "How long before she does something to us?"

I just shook my head.

"Now!" Dad said, while snatching the keys from Baker. "The grownups are back in charge. I'm getting these kids to Magnet City."

"And if I say no?" Baker asked, lifting the gun though not pointing it at Dad. The barrel faced down at a forty-five degree angle.

"Then I break your damn arm. I tell you what, Baker. You dump the ammo and you can ride with us to the next stop. We'll take you as far as Magnet City."

"You gotta be kidding."

"Dump it now, where I can see you. Then put that stupid thing away. If we run into Skulls, you can take it out and wave it around."

Baker sneered, and for a moment, I thought he'd refuse. Dad took a step forward.

"Okay, okay," Baker said. He unloaded the clip and handed the bullets to Dad.

Dad threw them toward the orange grove. "You and Kylie ride on the trunk."

I took Nolab from Mom, and felt him shaking. Grammy slid

over to make room for us, and Baker told Kylie, "I was tired of driving anyway." But he didn't seem in any hurry to get on the trunk. He and Kylie moved slowly, like they were waiting for Dad to change his mind. For the first time in their lives, they were the outcasts no one wanted for baseball or dodgeball, standing alone in the school gym, waiting for a team leader to finally grumble, "I guess... I'll take Baker."

I looked up into the sky, free of clouds and birds and bugs. And dogs. "Thank you for not taking Nolab," I whispered.

CHAPTER EIGHTEEN

Magnet City

From where we stood beside the Fleetwood, Magnet City looked like a traffic jam of buses waiting to get into the Magic Kingdom. Filling most of the main parking lot, the colorful tour buses, casino buses, and Disney shuttle buses formed a single curving line, bulging out before us like the outside wall of a sports coliseum. They were parked close enough together for their bumpers to be touching.

"Disney bought all these buses when air travel stopped," said Dad. "They thought they'd still get tourists to come."

The longer I gazed, the less real it seemed, mostly because of the stillness. Here we were, in Disney's main lot with no babies crying and no dads shouting, "We've got fourteen flipping hours in 90% humidity before the stupid parade. We need to pace ourselves." Off to our right, frozen in place, a three-car monorail glimmered in sunlight, while Cinderella Castle rose like part of a painted backdrop waiting for a play in an empty auditorium.

I took three pictures – buses, monorail, castle – each as lifeless as its subject.

"Like time just stopped," Grammy muttered.

We had parked about fifty feet from the circle. Dad walked slowly toward the buses. The rest of us followed. Borrowing Mom's survival idea, he tossed out pretzels to see if they wouldn't lift off. Each sank slowly toward the ground. There were no hidden pockets of Zero G.

"It's a spiral," said Jade. "The buses. They're parked in a spiral."

"I would've gone with circle," Dad said. "As in, circling the wagons."

Jade shook her head. "It's one long curving line all the way to the town center. It's a path, not a wall. The people here, they walk on top of the buses, using their magnets. The gap alongside the buses is a spiral too. It goes all the way. But if you enter that way, there are traps. Mama told us."

"How would she have known?" asked Dad. "Was she able to talk with your uncle?"

"They used to. Not lately."

We stepped onto the first of three dark metal plates placed in a row behind the last bus. Big enough to hold our car, the plate was streaked with rust like the highlights Mom used to put in her hair. "They used to use these in road construction," Dad said. "Covering trenches and sinkholes."

"I bet the spiral looks cool from the air," I said. "And not just like a long line of buses."

"Why don't you jump and find out?" Molly said.

"You first."

"It probably looks like a hurricane," Kylie said from behind us, "swirling around the eye."

Dad ignored us. "But *we* should be able to walk on top," he said, "since we've been Maintaining. That's got to be as good as strapping on magnets. We'll get the car and use it to climb up, make it our stepstool."

We didn't get to try.

"Stop where you are!"

Three men in metallic silver outfits glared down from atop the bus. The men were slim, and because they stood four feet above us, probably seemed taller than they were. They wore close-to-identical beards, brown and neatly trimmed, and shiny silver caps that covered their hair.

"We mean no harm," Dad assured the three men.

"We're hardly Skulls," added Mom.

"And you're hardly invited guests," said the man in the middle. A delicate silver chain barely stood out from the silver wrap that covered his chest. A red horseshoe magnet, maybe five inches wide, made up the pendant, its tips pointing down.

The other men wore similar magnets. Like crucifixes.

"What have they got on?" Molly asked. "Aluminum foil?"

I realized she was right. Though their pants seemed pretty ordinary, just jeans and slacks, the shirts and strange caps had all been shaped from aluminum foil.

"Doesn't it tear?" Molly said.

"Maybe it keeps them cool," I whispered. "Reflecting the sun."

Dad called up, "We rescued these children on the road. They lost their mother."

"That's very sad," said the man in the middle. "Now go on your way."

"Our uncle lives here," Jade said.

"We'll give him your regards," the same man replied. "It's not enough to get you into Magnet City."

"I want to see my Uncle Matthias," Jude said.

"You're testing our patience. Now beat it!" But one of the other men touched him on the shoulder. They turned their backs to us and talked quietly. I made out only "Not our concern" and "No one needs the hassle."

"Maybe we should leave," Mom suggested, but the men had stopped talking and were turning back to face us.

"Take them to the Reverend," instructed the man in the middle.

In an instant, foiled men were everywhere, pouring out from between the buses, poking, grabbing, and lifting us up. Fresh pairs of hands reached down from the bus top. I stopped jerking and twisting and putting up a fight, and soon found myself standing on the bus, surrounded on three sides by a whole new set of shiny men. "Dad?" I called out. "Mom? Molly?"

Jade stood a few feet to my right, but I couldn't see anyone else I knew.

Someone yanked my camera away, its strap burning my neck and ear.

I started to ask about Nolab, but figured he was safer in a car with windows slightly cracked. He'd been sleeping non-stop since the orange grove. "Proceed," said the guy who first gave the orders, and we started moving in slow, deliberate, and very loud steps. We sounded like wet cement in a mixer, more sliding than stomping, *smwoosh-plump*, *smwoosh-plump*. Jade moved closer.

The men had brightly colored backpacks attached to their legs. With images of Mickey Mouse and Cinderella's Castle, these drooped way down to cover their shoes. Jade said, "I'll bet they're filled with magnets."

"But wouldn't the magnets just stick to each other?" I asked.

Looking over the side, I saw one of the traps she'd mentioned before. Gooey looking dark stuff, like oil or tar or – I caught a whiff of un-flushed toilet – something super gross. It filled a long rectangular pit that stretched the width of the ground-level path, stretching from bus side to bus side. It looked like an effective way to discourage intruders.

"Hey," I heard Baker shout from behind me, "gun's mine!"

"Nothing is yours unless we say so."

"Leave him alone," came Kylie's voice. "He hasn't hurt anyone."

There was noise, commotion, then Baker saying, "Give it back."

"You better hope the Reverend's in a forgiving mood. Welcome guests bring gifts, not violence."

I hoped these words were intended for Baker alone. At least he'd been disarmed.

Molly, up ahead, kept looking back at me. I tried moving closer.

Some Magnet People, I saw as I squeezed past them, carried handguns of their own. I also noted that some wore nicer aluminum foil than others. The younger they were, the more likely their foil was crumpled or torn. Strips of Duct Tape tried to blend in without much success, like really old fashioned iron-on patches. Slipshod repairs for tears and holes. Not seeing any women or kids, I wondered what they wore. Or if there just weren't any.

"It's like the *Wizard of Oz*," Molly whispered once I got close. "But with a mutant army of tin men."

She took my hand. "Wouldn't you give just anything to go back to the yuckiest, most boring day before the Drop Down?" I could feel her hand trembling.

We walked a good distance, all of it slowly. Wherever the magnets were, they didn't make for mobility. Often, a deep crevice appeared before us: one bus ending and another beginning. None of these gaps stretched more than two feet across; mostly the bumpers were touching. Sometimes, wooden planks bridged the gaps. We crossed a total of sixty-two – after I started counting.

"Halt!"

The silver army stopped, and out came the hands, one more time, shoving us to the front. I saw Molly, Dad, Mom, Kylie, Jade, and Jude.

But no Baker.

The marchers dropped to their knees. "Reverend," they whispered in creepy unison.

Flanked on each side by five bearded sentries, a man in bright blue foil faced us. He stood on a pedestal of sorts – the bus's closed-shut roof hatch – but it added only inches to his height.

The Reverend was chubby, though hardly enough to make me think he'd been Maintaining. Mostly, he looked big in comparison to his skinny subordinates. If you put me, Dad, Molly, and Mom next to him, he might even have looked thin. He was also clean shaven, and didn't wear the foil cap. In its place flowed dark wavy hair like you used to see on TV weathermen. He wore eight gold rings, one on each finger.

"Uncle Matthias!" shouted Jude.

The Reverend's blue eyes gleamed. "Jade! Jude! Where is your mother!?"

CHAPTER NINETEEN

Song of the Sirens

Things got better fast, if like me you define *better* as drinking cold root beer from a frosted mug, served by slender girls who couldn't have been much older than me. Both – the drinks and the girls – appeared almost instantly.

We were still on top of the innermost bus. The girls were wrapped in aluminum foil that looked new, straight from the roll. They wore it like dresses, stopping just above their knees. They also wore smaller caps, making it possible to see most of their hair, pressed flat on their heads and held in place by some shiny gel.

I looked over at Mom, who was being served wine by two young men. She wore a super big smile, the widest I'd seen on her face since before the Drop Down began.

"Do you want more?" asked a cute red-haired girl, bending in close to refill my drink. Even though I'd already had plenty, the only answer that made sense to me was "Yes."

Jade and Jude were still hugging their uncle. "Once again," he asked, "where is my sister?"

"The Skulls," Jade said. "They chased Mama until she floated off."

Her uncle used some words I didn't think Reverends used, including a few that once got me grounded when I didn't want to mow our backyard. He went on, "At least you're here, safe in our city. Your mother was a good woman, and now she strolls the Golden Garden high above the sky."

He instructed two men to take Jade and Jude to his sitting room. "Treat them like the angels they are," he said. "I don't want to hear anything different."

They went down one of those rollaway staircases you used to see when people got off airplanes in old movies, and a few minutes later, we followed. This took us to the center of Magnet City, itself a pretty good sized circle, maybe as big as Carrolwood Mall. We saw lots of activity. Silver-wrapped people smwoosh-plumped past in all directions.

"A matter of protocol," Uncle Matthias addressed his new guests. "Only my niece and nephew may call me Matthias. To everyone else, I'm the Reverend."

The big metal plates were back, laid out side by side like tiles on a giant's bathroom floor. In the fashion of our hosts, we walked across these slowly, our root beer mugs clutched firmly in hand. Mom introduced our family. "And this is Kylie," she added, "Kylie Cho. She went to school with Adam. We don't really know the boy with the gun. He's been riding with us since Newton."

Grammy added, "Bit like a gnat you can't swat away."

I waited for Kylie to say something in Baker's defense. She didn't.

"We don't get a lot of visitors," the Reverend said.

"You don't seem to want them," said Dad.

"The congregation that followed from my old church kept growing and growing. You might say I had magnetic appeal. But even if rapid growth fit the business plan, it didn't take us long to run out of space – and we're talking months after my TV and webcasts disappeared with the power grid. Word kept leaking out, and folks kept pouring in. Friends of friends of friends, like when some innocent clown wins the lottery. You've heard about others sealing the exits. We had to seal the entrances. So consider yourselves the exception." He then raised his voice to request, "Magnetarians, some music, please! 'Welcome, Weary Pilgrims.'"

The crowd sang with one voice, hymn-like and strong:

Welcome, weary pilgrims all,
Make Magnet City thine.
Join our holy family here,
Hold firm, and always shine.

As we resumed our walk, I again noted the difference in foil costumes. Some of the women's were especially tattered. One man was getting his mended. A woman knelt before him, a roll of duct tape in her hands.

"What's with the aluminum foil?" Molly asked the Reverend.

"Ahhh." He smiled, wagging his index finger. "A popular question. But that doesn't mean I have to answer. Some mysteries are meant to be just that – mysterious."

As mysteries went, it didn't seem that intriguing to me. We'd learned about cultures and customs in school, and if these people wanted to wear aluminum foil, they could wear their stupid aluminum foil. Walking again, we passed Disney-themed double-decker buses and idling refrigerated trucks, their cooling units loudly humming. We passed fuel trucks, at least two dozen, which explained how the Magnet People kept the other trucks running.

"I thought I saw solar panels on some of the buses," Dad said.

"The Good Lord has blessed us," the Reverend said. "He has given us sufficiency in all things at all times. Food, fresh air, and fuel." When he showed us the water trucks, we heard pride in his voice. "Look at them, all ready and clean. That's why folks here don't smell so bad. Each tank is filled to the brim. We tapped into the groundwater."

"Is it safe to drink?" Dad asked. "I don't see any purification systems."

"You know what they say." The Reverend smiled. "What doesn't kill you will keep you alive a little bit longer."

We learned next that while some Magnetarians lived in modified trucks, most lived in the buses. They got in and out through the roof hatches, using chain ladders. Kids under ten went to school, which fittingly took place in modified school buses. Everyone else had a calling, whether collecting garbage or preparing food or repairing machines. "I could have gone with *chores*," the Reverend confided, "but *Calling* sounded more compelling."

Once we completed the tour, Mom, Molly, Grammy, and Kylie were shepherded by silver women to the fourth bus in the main spiral. The Reverend led me and Dad to a bus parked away from the others. This must have been his sitting room because Jade and Jude were there. Drapes hid some of the windows, and La-Z-Boy recliners had replaced the original seating. Halfway to the back, an electric fan rotated left and right from its base on the floor, creating a welcome breeze.

Dad and the Reverend sat up front where the driver's seat used to be. They each had a recliner, though neither chose to recline. The chairs were fitted with seatbelts; neither got fastened. At their feet, Jade skimmed through magazines: *Teen Vogue* and *Seventeen* in thick metal binders. Jude built a play city using real bricks.

The bus doors opened and a blond girl my age came in with Nolab in her arms. She put him down, and he scampered over to me. I smiled and looked over to thank the girl, but she had already vanished.

Dad was looking past the fan to the back of the bus. I followed his gaze to a ham radio station that looked a lot like ours had, if minus the towering battery packs. "That's quite the setup you have there," Dad said. "How come I never heard about you?"

"You probably heard us, just not about us. What's the point in attracting the rabble by advertising Magnet City?"

"The rabble?" Dad raised an eyebrow. "That's a fair stretch from weary pilgrims."

The Reverend laughed, showing a gold tooth. "Yes... them." The smile disappeared, replaced by a look of curiosity. "Do I know you from somewhere?"

"Unlikely," said Dad. "We're from just north of Tampa. Carrolwood."

"I've preached all over… before the craziness, of course. Wait a minute… I never forget a face… you didn't own a Radio Shack store?"

"Well," Dad said, raising an eyebrow.

"I needed a 15V adapter for my laptop. You talked me out of replacing the whole thing, just sold me the plug part. Six bucks total."

"And it worked?"

"You tested it and everything. I left thinking no one at the big box stores would've done that. You did me a favor."

Two young women, who in Full G world would have been going to college or working at the mall, entered the bus. Bearing Disney-theme backpacks and Reynolds Wrap, they crouched near the floor, trying not to create a distraction. In no time at all, they transformed Jade and Jude into Magnet People, their arms and upper bodies wrapped in foil, their ankles and shins strapped to the backpacks.

"Those can't be the magnets," Dad said. "Stuffed in a backpack, they'd just cleave to each other."

"The magnets are in our shoes," the Reverend said. "But the backpacks are important. Drooping around the shoes, they serve as buffers, containing the outward attraction. So we won't, as you noted, all stick together. As for the magnets themselves, you're talking cutting edge stuff. One powerful pull. The government designed the shoes, and was planning to issue them to every man, woman, and child until Lodeswirth pulled the plug. I offered to take the ones they already made. They offered an exchange."

"For what?" Dad asked.

"Throwing folks off the trail to NASA's Ark. I was one very influential person before the Drop Down. Prominent televangelist *and* cybervangelist. My Facebook page had one-million Likes.

The Pentagon's top brass requested I revise my sermon. For the Sunday before the Garbage Storms."

"They knew the Garbage Storms were coming?"

The Reverend ignored Dad's question. "They asked me to address the topic of NASA's Ark. 'Do we follow our faith or follow rumors?' I helped plant the idea that if there was an Ark it might just be located somewhere other than where it was. To keep folks away from the actual site."

"Which is?"

The commotion outside stole our attention. Four men in silver foil were carrying Baker, one man per limb. A fifth man in front held a black leash attached to what looked like a dog collar fitted tight around the prisoner's neck.

"You'll pay for this!" Baker shouted. "Every one of you!" He no longer wore his ballast. Gone were the laptops and flat-screen TV.

"What's happening?" I asked.

"Bringing weapons into Magnet City is a Class 3 Offense," the Reverend said. "We might cut him some slack, seeing he probably didn't know. But he must face the Airing of Accusations in order for this to be resolved."

"Maybe you should talk to my grandmother," I suggested. "She said Baker's done some pretty bad things."

"Outsiders are not permitted to take part in the Airing. Except the accused, of course. Bad things, you say?"

Baker squirmed and looked our way. There was no way he could hear what we were saying, but the look in his eyes gave me a chill.

"He might be a killer," I said. "You should ask Grammy."

"He's definitely got a temper," Dad said.

"I can see that," said the Reverend, getting up from his chair. "That boy has all the politesse of a rabid dog."

The Reverend went out, called to the men, and spoke. They listened and nodded.

Nolab curled up at my feet. A siren blared in the distance, not especially loud, but sudden enough to make me splash root beer onto my lap. I watched the Reverend turn toward the sound. The next siren was louder, while the third, a few seconds later, seemed right outside.

The first wail had surprised two of Baker's handlers enough for them to let go, letting his head drop slowly to the ground. They quickly regained their hold, and were back on their way, heading toward, then disappearing behind a refrigerated truck. The Reverend came back inside.

"What's with the noise?" Dad asked.

"Our warning system. The Skulls are trolling the Magic Kingdom."

Jade looked up from her magazine. "Skulls killed Mama," she said. "Chased her into the sky."

"Monsters," the Reverend said gruffly, clenching his jaw. "Every last one of them."

Jude slammed two bricks together. "They killed Mama."

"What do you mean, trolling?" Dad said.

"Fishing for trouble." The Reverend reclaimed his recliner. "They generally destroy a few things then get bored and go. You think of Disney World being neat and clean. But it's a real mess over there. Our sentries return with incredible reports."

"The Once Magic Kingdom," Dad offered.

"Originally," said the Reverend, "I thought we'd set up in there. But there were too many hiding places, too much ground to guard."

"You could have called it the *Magnet* Kingdom." Dad smiled at his own words.

"The havoc they wreak is quite amazing. Like they're striking back against their own messed up childhoods. After looting Main Street's souvenir shops down to the last candy bar, they managed to drag the Liberty Square Riverboat a quarter mile and wedge it into the arch of Cinderella Castle. And those lovable Country Bears… the animatronic singing group? Decapitated! Now tell me. Who does something like that?"

"Are we safe?" asked Jade.

"Of course we're protected. Whenever they try to breach our walls, we chase them away. They might think they're pirates or Vikings or whatever, but this bay's off limits."

A woman refilled my mug with frothy soda so cold it hurt. I took a second sip, enjoying the sting.

"How often does this happen?" Dad asked.

"Often enough. They control Epcot, though there's some question about how much time they actually spend there. They're still based out of Brevard."

"How do you know all these things?"

"Trust me," the Reverend said. "I have my eyes."

We heard shouts in the distance, punctuated by what must have been gunshots.

"What sort of punishment will Baker get?" I asked.

"Only what is deserved," the Reverend said. "But again, this is not a matter for Outsiders."

"Isn't he an Outsider?" Jade said from her place on the floor.

The Reverend used his hand to wave away the question.

"Your church?" Dad asked. "Is everyone here a member?"

"For the most part," said the Reverend. "We started out Deniers: me and my congregation. We doubted all the Negative Naggies."

"The ones who turned out to be right?"

"I don't concede that," said the Reverend with a sly smile. "After all, weren't they the same clowns who told us cigarettes and Big Mac's were bad for us?"

"They are bad."

"That's hardly the point," said the Reverend. "Try and keep up with me. As time went on, my parishioners kept floating off, and what's a shepherd without a flock? Driving back from Fort Lauderdale one day, I saw an alligator ascending. That's when I had myself an epiphany. Forgive me my blindness, Lord. What I have been witnessing is surely Your way. People, critters floating off all hours of the day. This is the Rupture."

"Don't you mean Rapture?" Dad asked.

"No, sir," boomed the Reverend as if Dad and I were part of a much larger congregation. "The Rupture. Different concept, different religion. With the Rupture, our bonds with the Earth are broken, letting souls rise to the Golden Garden."

"Then why is your flock holding on? Why go to all this trouble?"

"The Magnetarians will stay. The Lord has given His assurance. The atmosphere won't dissipate. At the very last, gravity returns and we inherit the Earth."

"We get the dirt?" Jude asked.

"Somebody has to," said the Reverend with that same knowing smile. "There are four trials. Water, air, fire, earth. Noah suffered the water. We endure the air. The other two are yet to come."

Dad looked down, probably trying to hide his smirk.

"I know you don't take me seriously, friend, but when was the last time you talked with the President of the United States one on one?" The gold tooth gleamed as the Reverend grinned. "Let me wager a guess… never?"

"We heard him on our ham," I said. "Just a few days ago."

"His double perhaps," said the Reverend. "You won't hear the real president on ham radio."

"An imposter?" Dad said. "Why?"

"Security reasons," the Reverend half-whispered. "To keep people calm. And in their own homes. Away from the Ark."

"Yet the president talks to you?" Dad said. "I didn't think Deniers cared for this president."

"He contacted me three months ago; wanted a read on

conditions down here. As for my current opinion of the Commander-in-Chief, you've got that part all wrong. Did you know he's the only one who knows the code to seal off NASA's Ark and make it space-worthy? He could've given the code to dozens of subordinates, but wanted to make sure his own reservation was secure, that the Ark could go nowhere without him. If nothing else, you've got to admire his survival skills."

"But someone had to give *him* the code," Dad said.

The Reverend shook his head. "They let him choose it himself, like it was a Facebook password."

"Well," said Dad, scratching his chins.

The Reverend smiled coyly. "With the president missing..."

"Missing? The president?"

We heard explosions, not exactly close, but not far enough away.

"They're ours," the Reverend said. "We're pushing them back."

The blasts continued. One sounded super close, rattling everything in the bus.

"If ever there was an argument for war, the Skulls are it," the Reverend went on. "They're also the reason the Ark's not fit to sail."

"Now I'm really not following," Dad said. "What do the Skulls have to do with NASA's Ark?"

The Reverend leaned back in his seat. "Why, Mr. Weaver, how much don't you know? They have the president."

CHAPTER TWENTY

Bottom's Up

Dad and I stood in the crowd that circled Baker's Condemnation Rite. It was early evening, the sky still light. Baker wore the dog collar and leash. His hands were tied in front of him. A large man in black clothes – foil free – held the lead's other end.

I couldn't see Mom or Molly or Kylie. But Grammy was nearby, escorted by two men wearing the more traditional foil wrap.

Baker still had one thing in common with the Weavers. No backpacks had been strapped to his ankles. No special shoes had been issued. That made us the only four without magnets. All around us, the Magnetarians talked quietly but excitedly. Like ancient Romans filling the Coliseum, they seemed anxious for the entertainment to begin. We heard words like "killer," "Outsiders," and "death."

"This might sound crazy," I said to Dad, "but only because it is."

He raised an eyebrow. "What?"

"We rescue the President. And he gets us on the Ark."

"But how?" Dad stammered. "The Skulls. You've heard what everyone's said."

"The same way we were going to walk up to NASA's Ark and convince them you left our tickets in your other pants."

Thanks to the Reverend, we now knew the Ark was in Cape Canaveral. "Leading people to Virginia," he had explained, "that was the ruse to protect the Ark. That's what they had me say in my sermon, that the Ark was at Langley." The eight-story office

123

building stood armored in six protective layers, meant to hold air pressure steady while minimizing damage from space debris, which was about to increase dramatically, when everything rose up. The outside layer was concrete, plopped on like frosting on a big square birthday cake. It had a clinic, garden, and water recovery system, meaning you could drink your pee. In deference to Biblical tradition, it boasted an entire Zoo-Farm Floor. It also had 400 human passengers, give or take a few. These were the "Regroupers."

The man in black snapped to attention. "All rise for Caleb the Elder!" he bellowed, ignoring the fact we were already standing. Directly across from us, a man maybe five feet tall emerged from a slim gap in the crowd. His thin rim of a beard was super white. His glasses were thick, in both their black frames and the lenses that turned his eyes into big dark balls. Wearing light green foil that looked brand new, he was the only Magnet person I'd seen close to Grammy's age.

Once in the center of the circle, he spoke quietly. But we heard every word.

"Raymond Bryce Baker, you faced the Airing of Accusations for bringing a weapon into Magnet City. You sought to cause hurt and harm. And who knows what would have happened had your gun not been confiscated? You still had two live rounds." I looked over at Dad who was bristling at how he'd been deceived. "Yet as serious as these charges are, they pale next to the weightier charges heard at the Airing. The Elders hereby condemn you for the Double Misdemeanor of bringing a weapon into Magnet City and for the Class 4 Felony of killing the residents of Newton Quality Care."

"I only helped them," Baker snarled.

"Silence! You injected others with lethal doses of drugs unfamiliar to you!"

"I did not."

"You selected these drugs at random," Caleb pressed ahead with a raised voice, "merely glancing at labels that meant nothing to you! The evidence has been weighed and a decision reached! You will now stand for sentencing!"

I could feel my heart racing.

"Consequently, you will leave Magnet City with the Outsiders who brought you!"

Now it was sinking.

"This can't be happening," Dad whispered.

"So where's my gun?" Baker asked.

"You're lucky to depart our city alive," said Caleb. "But it is not in our interest to waste space or food on incarcerating Outsiders."

That was when Baker saw Grammy.

"You witch!" he shouted, rushing at her. The man in black looked embarrassed to lose his grip on the leash. "What have you been telling these freaks?"

Baker didn't get to Grammy; I got him first. Colliding hard like a truck with a car, I knocked him backward a good four feet. "You?" he shouted while I took three swings, landing a good solid punch to his stomach with the last. "No fair," he protested, regaining his balance. "Fighting a man with his hands tied up."

He promptly jabbed with both fists, gouging deep into my belly. Forget fair. He was older and stronger. He was a monster. "You killed Grammy's friends!" I shouted, stepping back.

He charged forward, a head butt this time.

"Stop them, Reverend!" pleaded Caleb the Elder.

The Reverend said nothing.

"Watch out!" someone shouted from behind as Baker readied the leash to use as a whip. I lunged forward, plowing him into the crowd, which parted to let us keep brawling.

"No ball of blubber is taking me down," he snarled, shoving me away. But I could tell he wasn't so sure. He seemed as surprised as I was by my fury and strength. Maybe this last thing had come from living and moving in Low G, or maybe I'd always had it. Whatever the source, it was making me fearless.

"You're going to be sorry." He came back at me. "Sorry you ever started this." His fists connected with my cheek, which should have hurt more, but just seemed unreal, like I was watching it all in a movie or show. Until I tasted the blood in my mouth.

He turned and ran, which would have been stupid at half the speed. Even so, I moved just as fast, chasing him into the spiral that was the space between buses. I heard Dad shout from behind, "Stop, stop! One stumble you're dead!" But Dad must have been running too, because I heard his next words just as clearly: "Adam! The traps!" The path was paved with metal plates.

Windows blurred past. Out the sides of my eyes, I caught glimpses of faces pressed against glass, and it hit me how good, how incredibly good it felt to move like this, even with the risk of floating away. Was this how jocks like Q once felt when barreling down the field? Had there been more to sports than just being jerks and impressing girls like Kylie?

Catching up to Baker, I stepped on his leash, a move you couldn't make in football. This jerked him to one serious stop. He coughed a few times, got back up, and used one of his work boots to kick me where it hurts. "You're welcome too, fat boy."

Running again, he didn't go far; we faced our first trap. Rising like jagged fences, rows of wooden spikes stood three feet tall, level with vital organs. The spikes in each row rose maybe a foot apart. The rows themselves stood twice that far apart, reaching almost to the rear of the bus to our right. Even Baker must have realized that this trap had been designed to make intruders leap higher than needed and float off. He darted back to the front of the bus, and pried open the accordion doors.

"Ha," I shouted as he ducked inside, "you're trapped." There was no way the back doors would get him past the spikes. Climbing aboard, I took my time, sure I had him cornered. "Oh, hi," I said shyly, realizing I had entered somebody's home. Between two queen beds placed lengthwise against the bus's side – the left from where I started – a mom and two kids huddled together for safety. "You'll have to excuse me," I said walking past.

At the very back of the bus, Baker lay down, on his back, on a bench that stretched from side to side.

"Ha—!" His boots took aim at the last window. "Yourself!" Out it popped, frame and all.

"No!"

He flipped onto his stomach and slid through the opening.

I almost grabbed his leash. Almost.

"Great," I muttered to myself, accepting I'd have to push myself through the same window. Which is what I did. Feet first, stomach down, I didn't go quickly, or gracefully, or without help. Dad held my arms while I felt for the ground with my feet. "Don't ask me how," I said, "but Baker outsmarted me."

"You could let this go. Consider it a problem that solved itself."

"He made Grammy miserable," I said. "And the only thing that stopped him from killing her is that he thought she'd be useful."

"Be careful," he said as I took off on hard dry dirt. There were no metal plates on this stretch. Maybe twelve buses later, I reached the next trap. But I didn't see Baker. Extending the length of several buses, the barrier seemed impassable. Through a chain-link fence, five wild boars stared at me like they had not been fed in some time.

The bus to my right had its front door open. "You must be in here," I said, climbing onto the first step. "You—"

Baker flew out, diving at me. As I hit the ground, he got in a few more doubled-up punches. Tasting fresh blood, I kicked him away, just long enough to get back on my feet. Reeling, I felt dizzy. But that didn't stop me from landing a blow to his head. "Dead end," I said. "It's over."

"You got that right," he said, slamming me into the fence. "American razor-backs." He was trying to tip me backwards, over the top rail. "They're going to eat you like a candy bar."

I heard a loud grunt within inches of my ear, even felt breath on the back of my neck. "You know your pigs," I muttered. "I'll give you that."

"I know you, don't I?"

Mustering the little strength I had left, I slowly twisted free of his grip.

"And where do you think you're going?"

I shoved him against the rail. "Who's the candy bar now?"

"My old man used to hunt them," he said between heavy breaths. "Half million boars, all roaming free in Florida swamps. Now it's down to just them and you." And with that, he rammed me in the stomach.

I fell back a few steps, just as he leapt, aiming his fingers at a small metal ridge near the top of the bus. He was going to get on the roof and finish his escape. Moving fast, I grabbed his legs, but stumbled as I did so, losing my grip as I went forward. But I had pulled him away from the bus, aiming him more toward the sky.

I now watched from the cool ground. Baker was airborne, three feet and rising.

"Good God," he shouted. "Somebody help!"

To my serious disappointment, somebody did. Coming from nowhere to seize the end of his leash, Kylie cried, "Got you." But coiling the leash around her wrist, she too lifted up, a tail to his kite.

I pushed myself onto my knees. But no sooner had I grabbed one of Kylie's ankle weight-bands, I was rising too. I kicked my legs, thrashing wildly, feeling for ground. The boars grunted and squealed, loud; they seemed close. The top of the bus came into view, still maybe a yard away, too far to grasp. Not that I saw any parts fit for grabbing. A few more feet up, I made out Space Mountain, rising like the sun above the bus-top horizon. We were going to die.

Something gripped my ankle. "I've got you, son," Dad said. "Don't go anywhere." Momentum ceased, and… one-thousand-one, one-thousand-two… down I came. Mom had my shirt sleeve. A half-dozen Magnetarians, far from the safety of their metal sidewalks, stepped forward to help. I caught sight of Molly, jogging toward us.

I still gripped Kylie's weight-band.

"Thank God, Kylie," Baker said, and I knew she held his fate, in the form of that thick leather leash, in her hands. "I knew you wouldn't let me die."

"What did you do," she asked, "to get everyone so agitated? They didn't let me watch your trial."

"The trial was a joke," he spat from above. "Did you get a good look at those clowns all wrapped up like potatoes on a grill? Talk about crazy."

"Nothing, my butt!" Grammy said, breathing heavily as she came to a stop. "You killed my friends! You killed this girl's grandpa!"

"Not true," Baker shouted. "She makes things up."

"Did you kill my grandpa?"

Grammy called up to them: "He took away his meds. Switched them with crap not meant for him."

"These people were already dying. Time wasn't theirs to hold onto."

"They didn't ask you to hurry things up," Grammy said.

"I kept you alive."

"And killed everyone else."

Kylie must have readjusted her grip on the leash because Baker jerked upward an inch. "Hey!" he shouted down at her before countering Grammy: "We all would've died if we'd run out of food. Not everyone could live. Tell me, if there'd been fifty other residents at Newton when your family showed up, would your son here have found a way to get them all to the Ark? Would he have made ten trips to Virginia?"

"You should have just left us alone," Grammy said.

"They asked for my help."

"Nobody wanted your kind of help," Grammy insisted. "I still hear their screams."

"Fantasy! Lies!" Baker shouted. "Her memory's for snot!"

"Maybe so," Kylie said. "Maybe not." She looked down at Grammy's face, holding her gaze five very long seconds. "I know *I* have memory problems. They weigh me down more than gravity ever did. If anything, I'd like to be more forgetful. And all you do each time you open your mouth is remind me how tired I am of holding on, of holding onto this chain, of holding onto to everything."

A slight jerk backward. Had she let go?

"Kylie!" Up Baker went, slowly at first. "Kylie! You can't!"

I pulled her to the ground with help from Mom and Dad. "Well," Dad whispered into my ear, "that was quite the fight you had. A little pent-up anger can go a long way."

Molly squeezed in next to me. "I miss him already," she said.

"Don't you think you might have something you'd like to say to Kylie?" Mom asked her.

"Like she got the right person for once?" Molly said.

"You know what I mean."

"I know," said Molly.

But Dad spoke first, saying, "That had to be very difficult, Kylie," which had to be true since we could still hear Baker shouting, "You killed me, you worthless, conniving—"

"About those things I accused you of," Molly said, "I'm sorry."

"Thanks," said Kylie. "Thanks, everyone, for saving me." There were tears in her eyes.

"Like Dad said," I offered, "you did something super hard."

"It's not that... not *just* that... Grandpa, Mom, Dad... Q and his family... I feel so alone."

Mom gave her a hug. But Kylie pulled away, saying, "I think we should be going. Don't we have an Ark to catch?"

"We do," Dad said. He turned to Mom, and added, "After we rescue the President."

She looked like she was trying to get out a "What?" or something far worse.

"Sorry," he said timidly. "Adam has a plan, sort of. I'll let him tell you."

The Magnetarians helped lift us to the top of the bus, and we started back toward the center of Magnet City, following the spiral path. The sky was getting dark.

"We're going to the Ark first," I told Mom. "Let them know what we're planning, see how they can help us."

"And where is the President?" she asked. "Why does he need rescuing?"

"The Skulls have him," I said.

Mom's voice got louder with each syllable of "The Skulls?"

"You and Molly will stay behind," Dad said. "On the Ark. This wasn't your idea."

"That's assuming we get to the Ark," said Mom, "and assuming they let us inside."

"Assumptions are a big part of this," Dad conceded. "We're counting on some things going right."

Mom stared forward, expressionless. "Is that the whole plan?" she asked. "Not that we ever had much of one to begin with."

"We can fill in the holes as we go," Dad said.

"You rescued me," Grammy weighed in. "I never thought that

was going to happen. Never rule anything out, that's what I say."

"Just one thing," Mom said to Dad. "Please don't tell me you knew all this, about the President and the Skulls, before we left home."

"He didn't," I assured her. "The Reverend told us."

Molly slipped up behind me. "By the way, brother," she said quietly. "You were awesome."

CHAPTER TWENTY ONE

Next to Godliness

We ate as guests of the Reverend at a long table in a massive RV. "Hot quesadillas!" Molly squealed at one point. "With sour cream! Nobody wake me up! I want to keep dreaming!"

A girl dressed as a princess joined us for dessert: super sweet Jell-O cheesecake. A few years older than me, she had long reddish blond hair that was partly eclipsed by her princess headdress of purple and gold. Her white gown, accented by those same two colors, sparkled where it had sequins.

"I'm Felicia," she said. "Felicia Dey. I'm here in Magnet City because the Magic Kingdom was doing a play. A take on the old Ugly Duckling story. I was the Swan Fairy Princess. We were in rehearsal at the Town Square Theater."

"We've been there," I said. "Three years ago. On Main Street." It should have felt weird talking to someone dressed like a doll Molly once played with, but Felicia was a lot more animated. I tried to keep my eyes on her face, and not the gold and purple of her costume.

Felicia nodded. "Even after things got bad, Mom dropped me off every day. Most of the other kids showed up too. Stage moms are like that. They don't let a little thing like the world's end stand in the way of their plans. I never got to do the show, of course. I never got to be the Swan Fairy Princess."

I wanted to ask how she ended up in Magnet City, but she spoke first. "One Thursday in August, Mom didn't come back. I was stuck. Nowhere to go. The Reverend took me in."

Following dinner, she walked with me alone through the town circle. The air had cooled down, and if you didn't look up at the fluorescent lights fastened to metal poles, you'd have sworn the scene was moonlit. When she said, "Your fight may have been the bravest thing I ever saw," my cheeks burned and I turned away. She must have been watching from one of the buses; I wondered how much she'd seen. "That guy looked mean. And tough. But you didn't back down. Not one lick."

She took my hand, gently, like the breeze. "I reckon you could say Baker was handsome too. But in a crazy way." She loosened her grip. "Crazy handsome. I reckon some girls like that. It's probably better to settle for grounded." The grip tightened. "Especially these days. But he was handsome. I'll give Baker that. I guess he's in the Golden Garden now."

At the end of our walk, Felicia gave me a five-star present. She kissed me on the cheek, an action that would have earned four stars on its own if she hadn't bestowed it directly in front of Kylie.

"Stay strong," she whispered.

It's hard to explain how a bath feels when you haven't had one for months. Gross comes close, same for intrusive. It didn't help that darkness kept me from seeing the dirt as it actually clouded the water. I still felt the grit; it scraped against skin once shielded by grime. This took place in a coffin-like tank, metal below, metal above. The Magnetarian charged with my Cleansing told me the container had once been a sensory deprivation tank, "a crazy fad from years ago," words that sounded funny coming from someone wrapped in aluminum foil.

Mom, Molly, Grammy, and Kylie got the same treatment, or so I assumed. I only saw Dad when it came time for sleep. His clothes had been washed, same as mine, and we got super comfortable beds in Trailer Number Five. The Magnetarians seemed happy to have watched Baker secede from the Earth – and grateful for the entertainment we had provided in making that happen.

Nolab slept next to me. He fidgeted, kicked, and mutedly growled, sounding like Mom's electric toothbrush left vibrating on the counter. I wanted to believe he was having dreams as good as the ones I was having, but knew it more likely he was floating away, having twice come close during his waking hours. My dreams had me running across meadows dotted with flowers of every color. I was also being chased, but this was a good thing, since every time I looked back I saw Kylie and Felicia competing to see who'd catch me first. Cool air filled my mouth and lungs. I felt more alive than ever before. If only Nolab had stopped kicking me awake.

In the morning, our family returned to the RV for a breakfast every bit as unreal as dinner had been. The Reverend joined us for scrambled eggs, hash browns, steaming waffles with syrup, and grits. He and Dad must have already talked. The Reverend knew we were leaving after breakfast.

While he and Dad compared route options, Molly pressed Bow Wow Dog to her face, smelling the stuffed animal that must have been newly washed. Kylie flooded her southwestern omelet with hot sauce. She was more colorful than before, her weight plates secured with bands of bright blue duct tape.

Grammy was sitting with some Magnetarians. She smiled and laughed at things being said, especially when said by Caleb the Elder. When breakfast was over, she confirmed my suspicion. "I'm not going with you." She stood beside Caleb. The Reverend had joined their small group. "I like it here. I like the people here."

"You know gravity's not coming back," Dad said. "Your new friends are not going to inherit any planet worth having. No offense, Reverend."

"I wasn't born yesterday," Grammy said, "or even the day before. But I also know I'm not going on some shuttle bus to the moon. I lived my life. I just couldn't let it end in that vile stink hole of a nursing home. Here…" She smiled serenely as Caleb took her hand. "Much better."

"Well," Dad said, while Molly shrieked, "No, Grammy, no!"

"Are you sure?" I asked, but I already knew the answer.

"Molly, Adam. Always the concerned ones. But this doesn't change anything big. Let's just say I'd already figured out I was mortal before all this Drop Down foolishness."

After a good minute of silence, Dad said, "Reverend, you really can't tell us, why the foil?"

"Ah heck, why not." The gold tooth was shining, which meant he was smiling. "There's no grand symbolism, if that's what you're looking for. In our early days of Rescue and Reclamation, we came upon a warehouse in Edgewood, abandoned like every other business. The place was stacked ceiling high with pallets of aluminum foil."

"That's it?" Dad asked.

The Reverend cleared his throat, then began singing in a deep rich voice:

> *If we were in the open field*
> *The glare our foes would find.*

It was the same melody as "Welcome, Weary Pilgrims."

> *But should they breach our fortress walls*
> *The glare our foes will blind.*

The Reverend nodded as if waiting for applause. When that didn't come, he asked, "Mr. Weaver, could I borrow your son for a minute?"

Mom looked concerned.

"A minute, I promise. I just want to show him something."

The Reverend led me to his sitting-room bus. "Please," he said, pointing to the recliner Dad had used, while claiming the other for himself.

"You impressed me with your heroism, Adam, and I wasn't the only one." Leaning in close, he asked if I could keep a secret. And while I wasn't really 100% sure – not without hearing the secret first – I told him I could.

"We have a Chamber here," he said. "For withstanding the Rupture. Not forever, just till things change. And unlike that Ark, its doors will stay closed. I know your father would never stay, but if you wanted."

I started to speak, but he held up an index finger. "Think about it, Adam. Think." He reached behind his chair to pull out my camera. "No pictures, though," he said, handing it to me. "Not in our city. Not unless we know you are staying. Make that your choice, and you will have your own photo lab."

Back in the town center, I stood with my family in a circle, augmented by Kylie, the Reverend, and three Magnetarians. Molly stood to my right. "Where's Grammy?" I asked her.

She didn't need to answer. There came Grammy, her entrance providing one more thing that was hard to explain: how it was that she looked dignified in foil wrap. She walked close to Caleb the Elder.

Jade and Jude were following them. I stretched on my toes, looking for Felicia. I didn't see her.

We took turns hugging Grammy, crumpling her new foil a little each time. I held onto her for at least two minutes; it was hard to let go. "I'm going to miss you so much," she whispered in my ear. "You made me proud yesterday."

To Molly she said, "We sure are one good smelling bunch. Remember me that way, because this is how I plan to stay."

When Grammy bent down to pet Nolab, he came about as close as a dog can to smiling.

Jade and her brother soon stood before us. "We need to thank you for bringing us here," she said.

Jude offered Molly two bricks. "It's a puppy. I made it." That's when I saw Felicia, and boy, did I see her. She walked toward us in a fresh princess costume, silver, pink, and super shiny.

She stopped right in front of me. "You could stay."

"And you could come with us."

She pouted. "No. I can't. I belong in Magnet City."

I looked at Mom and Dad, looked at my sister. With a long sigh that seemed to release all the energy from my body, I said, "And I can't stay."

"Adam Weaver, I could make you very happy." She leaned into my ear to ask, "Did the Reverend talk to you?"

"You asked him to do that?"

"I want you to stay."

"I... I..." I looked over at Kylie, and saw the way she was glaring at Felicia, which certainly helped my resolve, if not enough. Felicia smiled. Her blue eyes lit up. Like Kylie, she was pretty and smart and interested in things. Unlike Kylie, she had never chosen Baker over me or almost let my dog float away. I looked again at Mom and Dad, and felt my heart imploding. "I've got to be with my family," I said.

"Oh my," Mom sputtered, and we looked up to see the roller coaster from Big Thunder Mountain in the Magic Kingdom. With its cow-catcher pointed straight at the sun, the Old West steam train slowly ascended, heaven bound.

"The Rupture," said the Reverend. "Picking up speed."

"Well," Dad said. "We should be going."

"You watch for the Skulls now," the Reverend said. "And if you run into Izzy McTell on some lonesome stretch of highway, you say hello for me."

"Izzy?"

"Goodness, Mr. Weaver, now you are putting me on. Everyone knows Izzy McTell fancies herself the Sheriff of Florida. It's best to stay clear, she's a dangerous person. Attracts danger."

"How so?"

"She's got a lot of weapons, for one thing. And then there's her constantly taunting the Skulls. Like when they sacked the Bullion Depository?"

"The Bully what?" asked Molly.

"Bullion Depository." Dad stepped in. "Better known as Fort Knox. Where the United States government stores gold."

"The Skulls took the gold," the Reverend continued. "They used it as bait for luring the President."

The explanation didn't make much sense, since contrary to every Doomsday scenario I'd ever come across in books, gold held no value in our world. As Dad liked to say, gold was worth its weight in weight, that and nothing more.

"So what does this have to do with Izzy McTell?" Mom asked.

"The Skulls robbed Fort Knox, and Izzy robbed them."

We fell silent, impressed by this news. The Reverend changed subjects: "You're only talking a two-hour drive to the Cape, even if you stick to the back roads we talked about. Lunch isn't all that far off. You could stay till then."

Dad looked at his watch. "It's true you shaved a day off our trip. But the Rupture's not going to wait an extra few hours for us, even with your connections."

Felicia stared at me, her sadness clouding the blue of her eyes. She held up both hands, and using her thumbs and forefingers, made the shape of a heart.

"My heart," she said. The hands moved apart, tearing that vital organ right down the middle. "It's breaking."

Before I could speak, the other Magnetarians joined together in song:

> *The Weavers came and we were blessed,*
> *With your presence gifted.*
> *You fought the worthy, holy fight—*
> *The evil has been lifted.*

Felicia moved her lips, and though I couldn't hear, I knew it was to whisper, "Stay."

CHAPTER TWENTY TWO

Noisemakers

With five of us inside and no one on the trunk, the Fleetwood felt less crowded. Mom sat up front, staring down another two-lane road. "Before we left home—" She placed her hand on Dad's knee. "You told us you had tricks up your sleeve."

"There are perks to running a Radio Shack," he said. "I put together some interesting devices."

"Like what?" Molly asked. Nolab slept on her lap, curled up like a puffy brown biscuit.

"Mostly devices to get us past crowds. For starters, I built a noisemaker so loud you've got to run for cover. I call it my Crowd Parter."

"That could be helpful," Mom said. "What else do we have?"

"There's what I call my Hot Gel. It sizzles with electric power. I don't want to use it, but if we're shoved into a corner, folks will back off."

"And for rescuing the president?" Mom asked.

"That…" Dad paused, "needs thought."

She removed her hand from his knee and turned to stare out her window. The car got very quiet.

Dad had not mentioned the device he'd installed with help from the Reverend's mechanics. This was his "Chimney," a powerful smoke machine meant to provide cover in a car chase. My guess was he didn't want to remind Mom that, thanks to the Skulls, car chases were now a distinct possibility.

Thinking we needed a new topic, I said, "Grammy was right.

We do smell good."

"A definite improvement," Dad agreed. "Even the dog smells better."

Molly sniffled, then burst into tears, prompting Mom to lean back and reach out to her. "What is it, Sweetie?"

"I miss my Grammy."

"Grammy's happy where she is," Mom said quietly. "Though she's going to get sick of that hymn."

"Amen," said Dad.

Lunch in an office park had me wishing I was back in Magnet City. Not even our cans of peaches and pears – let alone the processed cheese and crackers – could compete with fresh steaming waffles. We sat on a concrete loading dock beneath a metal awning that gave us shade; Dad and I had both left Magnet City with sunburns, which, as he explained, were easy to get in a thinning atmosphere. (Having our heads shaved helped, too.) From where we now huddled, we looked out across an empty parking lot, a deserted four-lane street, and a super wide lawn more brown than green. A pond – way too symmetrical to be anything but artificial – sat empty now, exposing the fountain heads that once sprayed geysers high into the air.

The one-story brick building behind it seemed every bit as lifeless and empty. Masterfield Press. Textbooks for the Future. Someone had covered the windows with plywood, like they once did for hurricanes. Looking around the office park, I saw the same on other buildings. It seemed hard to believe now that anyone thought life would return after the Food Riots. That was when these buildings would have lost their windows – looted for their vending machines by marauders who got a late start. But the plywood showed hope, a refusal to accept it was over.

"We should have asked the Magnetarians for carry out," Dad said.

"I bet they have great food on NASA's Ark," I said.

"Dining with the president," he said. "I should think so."

Molly coughed, spitting out crumbs. We watched these veer upward, staying together like gnats in a swarm. As they settled against the awning, Molly broke the hypnotic spell, "I can't believe Grammy stayed behind."

"Neither can I, Pumpkin," Dad empathized. "I liked the Reverend. But inheriting the Earth. That's not reality."

"And this is?" I asked.

"Adam's got a point," Kylie said. "Things floating away. Magnet People. A year ago, you couldn't have got me to see this as the real world."

Mom said, "Reality's just what you get used to. Back at the college where Dad and I met—"

"In Tallahassee?" asked Molly.

Mom nodded. "I took part in an experiment for psychology class. They paid us to wear special glasses that made everything look upside down."

Dad gathered up the empty cans and wrappers, and Mom waited for him to remind everyone we'd heard this story before. But he must have known better than to upset her again.

Mom continued, "The amazing thing is, after a few days, our brains corrected the image. Everything looked right side up again."

"You told us," Molly said.

"Which doesn't take away from the fact that Mom did something interesting once," I said. "Even if it was a long time ago."

"Thank you, Adam," she said flatly. "Never mind that I'm taking part in the most surrealistic road trip ever or that I nearly floated away in an orange grove."

"Sure real what?" Molly asked.

"When we took off our glasses," Mom resumed her tale, "everything flipped back over again. Like starting the experiment over, it took a few days for our brains to adjust."

She smiled. "A bit like the last six months, wouldn't you agree, watching our world flip a full one-eighty? It took some getting used to."

"That's the truth," I said, happy to see the smile. "I think back to stuff I used to do. Like going to Game Addiction at the mall. Those things seem upside down now."

"What I was getting at is this," Mom said. "We let Grammy wear the glasses Grammy wants to wear."

"You were really in that experiment, Mrs. Weaver?" Kylie asked. "I saw something about it."

"She had a headache for weeks," Molly said. "That's what she told us."

"We weren't the first to do it," Mom elaborated. "We were replicating results, as they say. But yes, I was in that experiment."

"Cool," said Kylie.

Moving again, I rode shotgun, stretching my legs whenever I felt like it. Nolab slept on my lap. Kylie sat directly behind me with Mom to her left and Molly claiming the left rear window. I didn't know what town we were passing when a rec center came up on our left. Its parking lot was packed with cars stacked three high. The cars in each bundle were matched by length, if not exact model and make. Color didn't seem to play a role either, except for one all-American midsize sandwich. A red Ford Mustang sat atop a white Chevy Camaro atop a blue Dodge Challenger.

The cars on the bottom of each stack appeared to be idling. "Skulls," Dad whispered, like they were going to hear him if he talked in a normal voice. "Eyes straight. Nobody stare."

I did as Dad said, looking straight ahead, which was easy enough since I felt frozen. Nolab perked up and was looking around. He seemed to sense the danger.

"They've got thick wires holding the car piles together," Molly said. "I count eighteen all together. I can see some of the men inside. They're really creepy looking. Like tattoos on their faces creepy."

"Didn't I just tell you to face forward?" Dad snapped.

"All you said was, 'eyes straight.' My head was turned sideways when you said it."

"Why aren't they doing anything?" Mom asked as we drove away.

"It is strange," said Dad, his eyes fixed on the center rearview mirror. "They haven't budged."

"This isn't good," Mom said.

"What were they doing?" I asked. "Studying us?"

"Studying us?" said Molly. "Why?"

I kept the answer – for future reference – to myself. I doubted they were just curious.

Lunch had succeeded in making me full. And sleepy. Dad drove and drove in a perfect straight line, like some mapmaker had drawn our road with a straight-edge ruler. Endless walls of pine rose on both sides. My eyelids felt heavy as magnets. I was falling asleep, drifting, diving...

"Good heavens!" Mom shouted.

A body dropped from the sky, plopping loudly onto the road's left lane.

"What was that?" Dad asked.

More bodies fell, like rain picking up. Some landed close to our car. Molly screamed. Kylie was crying.

"I don't believe it," Mom said. "The Drop Down's reversing."

"But these bodies," Dad said. "Where are they coming from?" A large one crashed down on our trunk, briefly tipping the car like a see-saw.

Soon, bodies were everywhere, fallen and falling. Dad slammed on the brakes. But only after hitting one very hard bump in the road.

"Impossible!" he shouted when Baker landed straight across our windshield. "There's no way!"

"Adam." Baker's voice boomed. "Bet you didn't think you'd see me again."

He pulled back a fist, ready to take out our windshield.

"Adam," Baker shouted. "You've got to wake up."

Molly was shaking me, hands on my shoulders. "Adam!"

Opening my eyes, I shook my head, hard and fast, the way Nolab used to when he got wet. But I couldn't shake loose the images of human precipitation.

"We've got trouble," Mom said.

We were stopped. Like in my nightmare.

A jagged cliff of triple-decked cars blocked the road. Same to our rear: more three-layer pileups. A dozen or so Skulls had already emerged from the car-wall up front. I could see they didn't Maintain; their bulk owed more to prison weight rooms. On top of that, they wore auto parts for ballast: mufflers and batteries, even what looked like whole engine blocks. I saw the tattoos. My sister had been right: the Skulls were as creepy as creepy gets.

And they were walking toward us.

I looked back at Molly. Pinching a clump of hair so that it looked like a Twizzler, she chewed on its tip.

Dad was holding the remote for his smoke machine. "Hold on!" he shouted, and our car screeched away, taking a hard left across grass that dipped down for drainage then into a supermarket parking lot. Aiming toward the storefront, we picked up speed, until we crashed through the empty metal frames that once supported sliding glass doors. Dad turned on the headlights, just in time for us to see the steel column that brought us to a painful stop. I heard moaning – my own. I heard Mom ask, "Is everyone okay?"

The Winn-Dixie's interior would have been plenty spooky

without the shadows created by our headlights. Great, empty shelves lay toppled on their sides. Broken glass sparkled like stars on the ceiling. Suddenly, I couldn't see any of this. Dad's "Chimney" smoke had rolled in like a fog. I started to climb out of the car, thinking we should run, but Dad told us to stay put. He was trying to back the car out, but it wouldn't cooperate. "Come on," he muttered, "come on, come on, come on."

The tattooed faces appeared, poking through the smoke to show off their Swastikas and barbed wire strands. The doors jerked open. Arms reached in to pull us out. I watched Mom and Molly curl up as one, Mom wrapping herself like a cocoon around her daughter. Refusing to simply surrender, Dad dove straight into the throng, all the while swinging wildly. "For God's sake, leave us alone," he shouted as they pushed him to the ground. "We're just a family." I followed his example, as did Kylie. Molly was dragged from the car, with Mom close behind.

The smoke made it hard to see, but also gave us some cover. We were all coughing. I felt my eyes water. Kylie and I helped get Dad on his feet. Like slow-motion fighters in a martial arts movie, we punched and kicked, easing our hopeless last stands toward the front of the store. Incredibly, I made it to the sidewalk, but all I could see through the billowing smoke were angry, ugly Skulls. No sign of Mom or Molly. Or Kylie.

An explosion rattled the ground, but not half as much as it rattled the Skulls. "She's here," one grunted with genuine terror in his eyes. The others looked away from us, like dogs distracted by squirrels.

I felt a tug at my sleeve, and turned to see Kylie giving me a look of "Let's go." I grabbed the back of Dad's jacket, and we snuck away through the smoke, getting as close to running as we could. Reaching the Walgreen's storefront, Dad said, "We need to go back. We need to find your mother and sister."

I only got out "I was thinking the same" before a loud, gruff voice ordered us to "Stop right there!" A tall, thin Skull backed these words with a bulky rifle, the kind we used to see in news stories about school shootings. Poking up in places like thorns, his orange hair looked as if it had been battered and stirred. His face was craggy, battle worn. A radiator from an antique car, worn like a vest, made up his ballast. Every inch of this had rusted orange, coming close to matching his hair.

"You boys are going back to see my brothers." He came closer, stopping maybe eight feet away. "Girlie here's gonna stay with me." He smiled to show off his dark yellow teeth. "Blackbeard's been taking everything for himself. Been a slew of blue moons since Artemis Cobb had me some companyship."

"Disgusting," spat Dad. "You're twice her age."

"And one-tenth her IQ," I added.

The gun was pointed straight at me.

"Listen, Artemis Cobb. I'm flattered to know you find me attractive." Kylie smiled as if she were flirting. "But you're never going to scare anybody like that. Not the way you're holding your gun."

"What are you talking about?"

Dad caught on before I did. "Are you crazy?" he said, turning toward Kylie. "Why would you tell him?"

"Tell me what?" said Artemis Cobb, his rifle now aimed at Kylie.

"A forty-five degree angle," she muttered.

"Stop," Dad sputtered. "No."

But Kylie continued, "You have to point the gun down at a forty-five degree angle. Otherwise the bullets go up into space."

"Yeah, and how would you know that?"

"One of our party died because he was careless with a gun," she said.

"Absolute truth," I added. "The effect of Low G on bullets."

Looking very unhappy with Kylie and me, Dad was showing his skill as an actor. "What's wrong with you two? You're just helping him kill us."

"Y'all, get lost. You can't fool Artemis Cobb."

I said, "If you don't aim low—"

"My idiot son," Dad muttered.

"You'll miss by a mile."

Artemis Cobb moved closer, narrowing the gap between the barrel of his rifle and Kylie's stomach.

"Is this here true? You better tell me, girlie. What all do you know?"

She lowered her eyes and shuffled her feet.

"Now!" he demanded.

"First of all, you don't want to shoot me," she implored. "I'm the one who tried to help you... but... a forty-five degree angle. It's true. You have to point the gun down at the ground."

"Suckers," said Artemis Cobb, backing off a few feet. "Girlie here was right. You ain't should 'a told me. 'Cuz I been thinking it might be best to kill these here boys."

Much closer than the first one, an explosion shook the Walgreen's storefront.

"Dang," said Artemis Cobb, his rifle now pointed in Kylie's direction. "What a time to run out of time. Now I'm gonna have to kill you all."

His trigger finger moved – and I charged at Kylie, pushing her aside as I heard the blast. I didn't feel pain, and hoped this meant I had not been shot.

"Look!" Dad held out his arms to stop Kylie and me. "It worked! He launched himself! He must have aimed downward!"

"You what-and-what so-and-so's." A fresh bullet created sparks as it grazed the pavement. Someone wasn't happy to be leaving the Earth. "Son of a—" His gun fired again.

Kylie, Dad, and I scattered, running different directions until Dad shouted, "He's drifted out of range. He's behind the Winn-Dixie."

I was hunched over, panting hard, when Kylie walked up. "Adam Weaver, you just saved my life."

"I *tried* to save your life," I corrected her, while using my sleeve to wipe sweat from my face. "But you beat me to it."

"Still…" Kylie leaned forward and puckered her lips, getting ready to kiss me. I closed my eyes and, more ready than anyone's ever been ready for anything, slowly leaned forward.

The air itself seemed to explode. Knocked to the right, away from Kylie and Dad, I felt huge slaps to my body, like waves, only harder, dragging me along the ocean floor – a fragile, teetering seashell, scraping rock and sand as I went.

Kylie screamed. I didn't know what was happening.

The last thing I made out through an eye barely open was the silhouette of a large woman on an elephant, elevated several feet above the ground, as if they shared a pedestal. In the swirling smoky haze, she looked like some Far Eastern goddess.

CHAPTER TWENTY THREE

Separation Anxiety

I regained consciousness at the base of a golden pyramid. The structure seemed to climb forever, but only because the sun's glare made it impossible to see all the way to the top. Still seated on her massive gray elephant, the large woman I had seen amidst the chaos watched over me. She used a Native American blanket – brightly colored in turquoise, pink, and brown – for her saddle. Silver spurs jutted out from her boots.

Nolab licked my cheek. I was lying on my back, aching everywhere possible.

"What happened?" I mumbled.

"He's alive." Another woman, somewhere to my left. "The boy is alive."

The elephant ambled closer, giving me a better look at the rider with slim silver sunglasses and super red lipstick, neither of which went with the pink puffy cheeks or wide soft nose. A yellow bandana covered her chin (or chins). Golden-brown ringlets danced below a white cowboy hat, while two leather gun belts, dyed the same brilliant white, had been buckled together to form one double-length belt. A few dozen holsters held guns and gold bricks.

Kylie's face soon eclipsed this view. She was pale and disheveled; her cheek was bruised. "Adam," she said, leaning in close, "thank God. I've been dying to tell you something. I was planning to… when we were alone. I thought I'd lost my chance."

These words sure sounded good, and more than a little promising. As I pushed myself into a sitting position, she straightened up, while stepping back to give me room.

"I'm sorry I let go of Nolab before. I wasn't thinking." She paused, looking deep into my eyes. "It was an accident. A stupid, stupid accident. I like dogs."

She stopped there, without adding something like *I've always been secretly in love with you. I dated Q to make you jealous.* I said, "I'm glad you like dogs." I was getting on my feet.

"Um… Adam, you might want to keep sitting," she said a bit too late. "There's something else you need to know."

"It's okay. I'm good." I couldn't help but stare at the pyramid, blazing in sunlight. From my new perspective, it still seemed huge, especially when measured by the number of gold bricks that must have gone into constructing it. The structure stood maybe three stories tall. I noticed something else: the moist, rank smell of a zoo or county fair. This actually brought comfort, if only because it held some familiarity.

Kylie had waited a few seconds before resuming, "Your dad's here, but still asleep. And no one's seen your mom or Molly. They're assuming the Skulls got them."

"Mom? Molly?" For the first time in months, I felt heavy. My legs had trouble supporting me.

"So this is the Fort Knox gold reserve." Dad was up, sitting cross-legged. His face showed plenty of cuts and bruises, like mine probably did, and he looked like he could pass back out at any second. Our hosts had given him water. I wasn't sure how or when to tell him about Mom and Molly. It was clear he didn't know; he seemed almost cheerful. "All I can say is you've got one very nice house."

"I got lucky really," said the woman who had been on the

elephant. Though the cowboy hat made it hard to be sure, she seemed about Mom's age. "A year ago, I could never have afforded it."

"In many ways—" Leading a camel by rope, another woman emerged from behind the pyramid's corner. Her short dark hair and jet-black sunglasses looked like a single hard object made out of plastic, using one mold. The camel had two humps. "The Drop Down's been good to us."

"The first few weeks were fun," added the elephant woman, "I'll give you that. As a full-figured woman, I sure didn't mind watchin' everyone who'd ever ragged on me bite the big cloud. Sayin' Happy Trails to the morbidly thin." She paused before adding, "Until it got lonely." Looking back at the woman with the camel, she continued, "You ask me, the Drop Down's been a bit of a bust."

The elephant and camel weren't the only zoo animals walking the grounds bordered by a high golden wall. I saw zebras and giraffes, a couple of bighorn sheep. Wearing lumpy harness bags probably stuffed with more gold bars, they seemed oddly at home among the military tanks and heavy-duty construction vehicles. There was a long flatbed truck, its rear connected to the ground by a gently sloping metal ramp. Was that how I'd seen the woman and her elephant back in the madness? Had they been riding on the truck's bed?

"So what exactly happened in the Winn-Dixie?" Dad asked, pushing himself to his feet. "It was how a drum solo must feel..." He rubbed the back of his head. "To the drums."

A rhinoceros grazed on tall, thin plants that grew in bright green clusters. The elephant woman noticed my watching. "We rescued all these beautiful creatures," she explained. "Those vile Skullectors were hosting barbecues in zoos and wildlife preserves. That was when I started taking things from them."

"Well," said Dad, "then thanks for adding us to your endangered species list. You must be Izzy McTell."

"Isabelle by birth, grew up Belle McTell. I got tired of that right quick, I tell you." She shared a few details from life before the Drop Down. As Chief Librarian in Broward County's Fort Lauderdale branch, she loved reading real-life histories about the Old West. Pearl Hart... Kitty Leroy... these women had been heroes to her. "As you might have noticed, all that stuff came in handy when the world flipped upside down."

"She doesn't like Belle as a name," said a third woman, coming up on Izzy's left. Her head was shaved completely bald, at least where her sky-blue cowboy hat let us see it. She didn't seem to be associated with a particular animal; she wasn't escorting a hippo or walrus. "But get this: Izzy here chose the town of Belle Glade to homestead our Pyramid A Ranch."

"Belle Glade?" said Dad. "That puts us south on the map."

"Sugar cane capital of Florida," said Izzy. "Known for its fertile soil, uncharitably described by some as muck. We're right off Lake Okeechobee and the Everglades. We are, in fact, directly across State Road 715 from what used to be the Everglades Farm Equipment store."

"So where are you keeping my wife and daughter?" Dad asked.

The bald woman offered Dad a silver flask, which wasn't good. As unflagging as his momentum seemed to others, it was in reality a fragile thing. Bad news, followed by a shot of whatever was in the flask, would slow him down, and Dad had to keep moving at his usual speed if he was to move at all. I knew this from watching him give up on his Wire Detangler.

"Am I going to need this?" he asked.

It was Izzy who nodded.

"Well?"

When Dad got his answer, he muttered and paced. "We need to find them. Now… No Skullector's going…"

He did not take a drink.

"Did our car make it back?" he asked, and Izzy led us around the pyramid's corner. We saw the Fleetwood. It looked pretty banged up. All the ballast on top was gone, ham radio included. The trunk lid pointed up, already open. The Skulls had taken our food.

Dad's hands disappeared inside the trunk; he was sliding things around. "I guess they didn't get everything," he said without much life in his voice. "Almost all of the small electronic stuff is still here. Maybe they figured it was worthless junk."

"Or maybe they got distracted," Izzy boasted. "I think we deserve some credit here."

"Maybe." Dad looked ready to cry. Not that I wasn't ready to join him, knowing the danger Mom and Molly were in, combined with seeing him this way, not just beaten up, but beaten down.

"They figured wrong," I said, trying to fake some conviction for his sake. "That worthless junk is going to help us save Molly and Mom and get us on the Ark." Peeking in through the car's back passenger windows, I saw no cameras or violin cases. "We're going to beat those animals."

I tried to pat Dad on his shoulder. He moved away.

"Remember the baseball?" I said. "Remember watching it shoot up out of sight?"

He didn't say a word.

"Not that first one at the game. The other one." I stepped in front of Dad, which put us face to face. He didn't look away. "The one in our backyard," I continued, and I swear I saw the faintest trace of a smile – and the dad I knew. "Out of the park. That's what you shouted as it disappeared."

"I did," he said faintly. "I did hit that ball into the sky."

Stepping between me and Dad, Izzy McTell told us she wanted to help and would do what she could. But time was running out, along with any hope. No one was getting on the Ark. "I feel bad for you and your family, just like I feel bad for everyone. But trust me. We learned this the hard way." She and her posse, she explained, had long planned to be onboard when it rose up. But that meant rescuing President Lodeswirth, which was where her plan stopped, "hitting that proverbial wall." Izzy knew where he was, and it wasn't Brevard Correctional. The Skulls had taken over a bowling alley in nearby Melbourne. They were firmly entrenched, held all the cards, and could easily kill the president if Izzy showed up looking for a fight.

"What if *we* rescued the president?" I asked.

"You and whose army?" scoffed the posse member with black molded hair. She smiled coldly, which fit her overall iciness.

"I was thinking… United States."

The bald woman joined her in laughing at me.

I spoke louder. "I have an idea. We go to the Ark and enlist their help in tricking the Skulls. What does anyone on the Ark have to lose? They need the president back."

"Why would they even listen to you?" the ice queen asked. "There are lots of people trying to get their attention."

"I don't know. I just know we need to rescue my sister and mom." Thinking quickly, I added, "Mom was a librarian too."

"It sounds hopeless," said Dad, "impossible."

He gave me a look to match his words. Sorry, son, it's over. His eyes were wet and red; I couldn't blame his allergies. That was when it really sank in: we weren't going anywhere. Molly and Mom would never escape, and NASA's Ark was doomed. But then Dad did something to confuse me, something akin to squirting lighter fluid onto a fire at the same time you're dousing it with water. He handed the untouched silver flask back to the bald woman.

"Your pa here has a point," said the woman with molded hair. "The whole thing sounds crazy. So I'll ask you again, How are you going to get past the crowd and moat?"

"Have you ever been in a Radio Shack?" Kylie surprised us all by speaking up.

"Not recently," said Izzy McTell.

"Mr. Weaver invented their biggest selling product."

"That's right," I said. "Wire Detangler."

Dad gave me the strangest look, half proud and half sad.

"No offense," said Izzy, "but right now he don't look like no famous inventor. More like some dreamer who tried driving across Florida to get on the Ark but instead got stopped by the Skulls."

"Wait," the bald woman said, "I've heard of Wire Detangler."

"That doesn't mean he's got some brilliant plan to get on the Ark. 'Cuz if he did, don't you think he might'a used it?" The woman with molded hair turned back toward Dad, me, and Kylie. "So I'll ask you again, how do you intend to get past the crowd and the moat?"

"With this," Izzy McTell announced. She reached up under her T-shirt to fetch a black three-ring binder. Strips of masking tape hung off the sides, which must have been binding it to her body. "I've been holding onto it – my Ace of Spades as it were, hidden up the sleeve."

RESEARCH PROJECT 47839384545, read the gold embossed cover, NOT FOR DISSEMINATION. PROPERTY OF THE UNITED STATES DEPARTMENT OF DEFENSE.

"This is what the Skullectors used to lure out the president," she said. "It wasn't the worthless gold." She opened the binder to show us mathematical formulas, printed in small type that went on for pages. These used as many letters as they did numbers, along with dozens of strange symbols that might have come from other languages.

"It looks like a cat walked across a keyboard," Kylie said.

"What's this?" I said. "Spin-2 boson. Second-rank tensor. I've seen those words before."

"We believe there are formulas here for producing microgravity," said Izzy McTell.

The wildlife grew restless. The rhinoceros grunted. We heard what sounded like firecrackers – or guns – followed by a huge, ground-shaking explosion. Dad's head jerked sideways like Nolab's used to whenever he saw a rabbit in his yard. "Skulls," he said.

"Nah," said Izzy McTell, "just Raging Miranda. She likes blowing things up. You can thank her for your rescue – and current existence. Those useless Skullectors know better than to come anywhere near here. Miranda ain't content to just give them concussions."

"Rae Jean?" asked Kylie.

"Ra-ging. They used to call her Cheerful Miranda, back when she served as a munitions expert at MacDill. She was in her element there. But when things got crazy, so did she."

Izzy told us more about the Ark. Months ago, the mob surrounding it was thousands strong. Now, she estimated that fewer than 200 people remained. "Attrition," she said. "That's the nice way of putting it." Not that it would be easy getting past what remained of the throng, where desperation had increased in reverse proportion to the loss of population.

"The moat?" Dad asked.

"A stretch of powerful spring-loaded plates that pop up to launch the uninvited," said the bald woman. "There are hundreds of them."

Izzy spoke: "It's our reckoning the Skullectors wanted you to deliver a message for them."

"Which was?"

"The vice president needs to rethink his position. That's if he wants to see the president again in this life. Messrs. Blackbeard and Plumm, you see, reached an impasse some time back. The Skullectors were demanding admittance to the Ark in exchange for the president's safe return. That would have given them the Ark. In making room for the Skulls, almost all the Regroupers would have to be expelled."

"And I was to be the messenger?" Dad asked.

"One of them," she said. "It's the toll for crossing Florida these days."

While Dad took this in, I asked, "The binder? You're really going to give it to us?"

"I am," she said, "and you're going to get me and the gals on NASA's Ark."

She quickly added, "You do have a plan to rescue the president?"

"We made it this far, and—" I looked at my dad. "We've got a genius inventor."

"You don't have a plan."

"We'll have one," I said. "You've just got to trust us."

Kylie added, "Unless you've got someone better."

CHAPTER TWENTY FOUR

Izzy McTell had a strange way of contributing to our mission. She kicked us out. Goodbye. Good riddance. "Blackbeard doesn't care much for me," she explained. "The sooner you move on, the more likely he'll think you're doing his bidding and not mine. We can give you food and other supplies. The good news is your trip's a short one."

She told us that, starting the day after next, her posse would be waiting for us at the main NASA gate. "Once you return with Lodeswirth, we expect to be repaid for giving you the binder."

She let Dad use her ham radio before we left. "You might have to plug the mike back in. We only use our ham for eavesdropping. We need to know what others are up to." Her set-up occupied the center of a patio laid – big surprise – with real gold bricks on the pyramid's far side.

Dad held the microphone close to his face. "Reverend," he said, "I don't expect a response. But I need you to listen. We've run into trouble. Incurred losses. We're down to three. It's imperative we succeed. We should reach target near 10 a.m."

He stayed on the ham maybe ten minutes more, but couldn't make contact with any of his old buddies. No Michigan or Alaska. When an elderly woman's voice intoned, "Yea, though I walk through the valley of death," Dad handed Izzy the microphone and started toward the car.

Our Fleetwood looked like it had puffed up from some weird allergic reaction. Sixteen recyclable Whole Foods shopping bags bulged out from its sides, each one packed full of gold bricks and fastened in place with metal screws.

When we drove off, Izzy called after us, "Don't trip up."

By the time we reached the beach towns near Cape Canaveral, the world was growing dark. "Over there," Dad said, pointing to the two-story parking ramp that separated Souvenir City from a restaurant promising "Snow Bird Special Early Bird Dinners." The dull-white buildings looked like ruins from a long-ago war, the windows and doors smashed out. The parking ramp, in contrast, looked unscathed, the bunker no bombs could touch. "If we drop anchor there, so to speak, we'll be safe from drifting off."

I didn't ask, Wouldn't the whole ramp lift off in Zero G?

Sleep came in spurts, punctuated by visits from Baker and Grammy and Skulls with guns. Each time I jerked awake, I felt Kylie's head on my shoulder, reminding me that hope wasn't useless. Maybe we would get into the Ark. Maybe we could rescue Molly and Mom.

The one time I got up to pee, I walked to the edge of Parking Level One. And leaning out over the low concrete wall, I was overwhelmed by the universe. So many stars shone against absolute blackness, no streetlights or moon to subtract from their power. They seemed to assure me, "Everything's fine out here where we are, or at least it was 50,000 years ago when we sent out the light you're seeing tonight."

Kylie came up on my left. "Trouble sleeping?"

I jumped a little but was able to smile, if only just barely, glad I'd finished going to the bathroom before she surprised me. "I was thinking about Mom and Molly," I said. "I'm way more scared for them than I ever was for myself."

"We're going to rescue them," said Kylie.

"I know I told Izzy we'd trick the Skulls, but how is that possible? I mean, really?"

"I don't know," she said, "but if I've learned anything from this trip, your family is good at outlasting crises."

I said nothing.

"I don't think I told you, but your mom reminds me of mine," she whispered.

"How?"

"Independent, proud. A few years back, she swapped housecleaning duties with a friend from another suburb. They cleaned each other's houses." Turning, I could barely make out Kylie's smile in the dark. "We didn't have much money. Ma did it to make our neighbors think we could afford a cleaning service."

I didn't tell her I could never imagine Mom doing something like that. If anything, it sounded like a Dad idea. So I just said, "She never liked our little house. I was always surprised we didn't move into one of the big empty ones after the Drop Down got bad."

We stared at the stars another few minutes. "We should get back to sleep," she said. "But I need my pillow."

Just after nine the next morning, we were crossing the inland waterway, which meant we were close to NASA. We looked down on the sparkling blue Indian River from one of those long Florida bridges that reminded me, with its four lanes split evenly into pairs, of two wide silver ribbons unrolling.

"I've been here before," Kylie said. "With my family. We took both of NASA's half-day tours. Each one lasted a half day too long. Don't get me wrong. Space travel was amazing. But we just saw graveyards. 'Here, in that empty space between the pines and palms, is where the shuttles used to take off...' 'The lot to your right is where the Apollo launch pad stood...'"

"We came here too when I was little," I told her. "I don't remember much except for Dad buying me a model of the Explorer Shuttle. I remember watching him build it back home."

"It all seems so strange," she said. "There should be birds everywhere. Pelicans, egrets. You wouldn't know we were close to the ocean."

"Did you see that?" Dad asked.

"Still do," I said, as my eyes followed the wriggling flash of silver upward. "It's no bird, but it sure is soaring."

"A flying fish," Dad said. "He probably came out to see where all the bugs went."

"If that's true," I said, "he found out."

Off to our right, a second fish followed the first into space.

"Well," Dad said as we came off the bridge. "Well."

Dry land wasn't so dry. Where river stopped, swamp began. But still no birds or other creatures.

"Where's the Visitors' Center?" Kylie asked. "Shouldn't it be right over there?"

"I took the long way," Dad said as a sign welcomed us to the beach town of CAPE CANAVERAL. "We're circling around from the south and east. To avoid the gate crashers."

I said, "Don't you mean the other gate crashers?"

Maybe five minutes later, we turned into the parking lot for Jetty Maritime Beach. "I was planning to stop here all along," Dad finally explained. "A surprise for your mother. I thought we'd snack, then proceed to the Ark."

"Why stop now?" Kylie asked.

"Because I owe it to her." He waited a few beats before adding, "And to get things ready."

Outside the car, we stood over the open trunk. Dad pulled

out a coil of rope. "Tie this to your wrist," he said, walking to a guardrail meant to keep drivers off the beach. "We can't go floating away after making it this far." Bending down on one knee, he secured one end to the barricade.

Soon, I was looking out on a different kind of eternity from the stars the night before – and wishing I still had my camera. I would have tried to preserve the majesty of what I was seeing and tasting and feeling: the ocean's immensity; the saltiness of the breeze; and the anger of waves as they collapsed, one after another, beaten down by the shore they had started out thrashing.

"I hate to say this," Kylie interrupted my thoughts as she walked up beside me, "but this is disappointing." And with those words I saw the beach more clearly, and not through lenses clouded by memory and images from movies. The ocean still went on forever, of course, and the air tasted of salt. But the waves seemed small and pathetic, their anger issues long resolved. They lapped the shore with much less force than when the moon created tides.

I heard a sniffle and turned to face Dad. He said, "She didn't want to come. She didn't even want to come."

"But she came, Dad. She came for us. And now we're going to save her."

When a stingray lifted from the water, continuing up in a perfect straight line like a sleek gray fighter jet, Dad said, "We should probably get organized. Adam, Kylie, could you help me with something?"

Standing beside the Cadillac's trunk, I watched Dad pull out the first Radio Shack box. "I wish your mother could see this," he said. Then, we were on our knees on the warm asphalt, assembling the "Crowd Parter" he'd mentioned before. Kylie and I helped unbox an electronic horn, three cone-shaped speakers, a couple of amps, several more preamps (he had to explain what these did), and lots of wire and tubing. He used black electrical tape to help assemble his creation, and sharp metal screws to secure it to the roof. Once he was finished, the car looked even more like something out of a Dr. Seuss book, all loops and wild shapes.

He reached into the trunk and handed me a black remote, like we once used all the time. Handing it to me, he said, "Just push Play. But only for a second."

The blast that followed – part air-raid siren, part fingernails on blackboard – almost knocked me over.

Nolab, the ever quiet dachshund, howled along. "Dad!" I shouted. "I think it might work!"

He turned away and sneezed three times.

Back on the road, we crossed another long bridge, this one spanning the Banana River. JOHN F KENNEDY SPACE CENTER, a sign announced. ADMINISTRATIVE AREA. AUTHORIZED VEHICLES ONLY. A security gate lay on its side like the barbed-wire fence that adjoined it. Beyond that toppled boundary, we saw what looked like a mall parking lot right after a tornado, with cars and trucks thrown every which way.

"I can still see the main road," I said. "They must use a plow to keep it clear."

"A big one," Kylie noted.

We continued slowly while staring in awe at the parallel mountain ranges rising a good fifteen feet on both sides of our valley. "All these abandoned cars," I said. "We're hardly the first ones here."

"Like toys," Kylie said, "shoved out of the way."

"We're looking for the Administration Building," Dad told us. "I believe that will be the Ark."

"Any chance it's behind that wall of people?" Kylie asked.

"Well," said Dad, "NASA's Ark."

CHAPTER TWENTY FIVE

The Ark

A wave of disappointment washed over me as I took in NASA's Ark, a reaction that surprised me since I couldn't say the Ark was much different than expected. But this didn't change a simple fact. When reading my books about space wars and adventures, I had imagined myself sailing the night sky in all kinds of strange, fantastic crafts. This didn't look like any of them.

What it did look like was a basic eight-story office building that had been crapped on with lumpy cement – the last of its six protective layers. I must have made my observation out loud, because Kylie disagreed: "You're crazy. It looks like a birthday cake."

I looked again and saw how the concrete had flowed down the sides creating different shades of gray, like vanilla frosting with a bit of chocolate, not blending very well. Rocket boosters on the roof, positioned upside down, gave the cake its candles.

Dad was focused on the mob. "At least Izzy was right," he said. "There can't be more than a few hundred people."

"It looks like a centipede," Kylie noted, "with hundreds of legs."

Dad said, "Time to see if our little toy works." We had reached the edge of the crowd. "Full power this time."

"That wasn't full power back at the beach?" Kylie asked.

He reached beneath his seat. "Here," he said while holding out pairs of big clunky headphones, "we're going to want these on our ears."

In the backseat, Kylie put her headphones on, then bent over to cup Nolab's ears. Curled up beside her, he didn't protest.

Dad offered me the remote. "Want the honors?"

"No, Dad. It's your invention."

"Okay," he said quietly. "Three, two…"

Suddenly, I was glad to be wearing the headphones. The huge piercing noise hurt even with them on, so it must have really hurt the people outside our car. They sure wasted no time in covering their ears and backing away.

Driving quickly through the canyon they created, we saw woman after woman and man after man glaring at us. I stared myself, unable to look away from these huge individuals with compact refrigerators, garden gnomes, and even kitchen sinks strapped to their bodies.

Ever so briefly, I thought I saw my English teacher, Ms. Hardman. But the chance that she was still alive hardly made me smile, not if she was part of this sad mess. What hope did they have of getting out alive? Of course, they could have been asking the same question of us as we passed.

Hands hiding his ears, a man wearing an old steam radiator for a vest charged the Fleetwood. Dad grabbed the remote, pressing a button. A thick yellow foam sprayed out on both sides of the car. This must have been the electrified gel because the man screamed, slid to a stop, and retreated. Dad's lips moved to say, I think, "Sorry."

We emerged on metal plates very similar to the ones at Magnet City. A couple hundred feet still separated us from the building, which was circled by soldiers. Heavily armed and squeezed into camouflaged uniforms that no longer fit, they stood shoulder to beefy shoulder, maybe three rings deep. If the Ark had an entrance, they blocked it well. We couldn't see any doors. All we could see were the portholes, higher up the walls. These were the only windows.

There was one more layer of protection. A few dozen tanks were scattered here and there between us and the soldiers. Painted in either dark green or desert-sand beige, their colors made the massive yellow bulldozer, standing two stories tall, stand out even more. It must have been used to keep the road open.

The Crowd Parter stopped squealing as we came to a halt halfway between the mob and the Ark. Dad said, "We're on the moat," a theory confirmed when a woman wearing what looked like a small outdoor fireplace darted out of the crowd, maybe 50 feet to our left. One of the metal squares popped up sideways like the lid of a Jack-in-the-box, launching her skyward at a pretty good clip. I wanted to look away, but couldn't, no more than I was able to block out her scream. Its work done, the plate dropped back into place.

Mounted high on the Ark's front wall, a gray surveillance camera that would have been right at home outside an entrance to Carrolwood Mall followed her path. Satisfied that she was gone, it lowered its gaze toward us.

"I don't think we should move," I whispered.

I had not been watching Dad, but saw him now, clutching an electronic bullhorn as he climbed out of the car. He stood behind the open door, leaning forward on its rim.

The bullhorn squealed for a second, then let Dad make a highly distorted request, with each consonant producing the sound of metal scraping metal: "We need to *kkkhh*-speak with the *kkkhh*-highest ranking *kkkhh*-official!"

The soldiers didn't react.

"We *kkkhh*-need to speak with the *kkkhh*-highest ranking official!"

Dad repeated the request three more times.

Finally, he got a reply: "You wish to speak with the President of these United States of America?" This came from a gray loudspeaker mounted on the Ark's wall. "Insolence!"

From the corner of my eye, I saw the mob move back slightly. When I turned to get a better look, dozens of curious eyes returned my gaze.

"We know *kkkhh*-he's not *kkkhh*-here!" boomed Dad's distorted voice.

This was followed by silence. Then: "We can't help you!"

"But we can *kkkhh*-help you!" Dad responded.

This was met with more silence.

"We! Can! Help! You!"

"Nonsense!" the Ark replied.

"We have several things of-*kkkhh* value to you! Beginning with information! A certain leader's whereabouts!"

I don't think Dad noticed the shiny white tour bus pushing through the crowd like it didn't care who stayed or jumped out of its way. I don't think he even saw it coming to a stop directly behind our car. Because he sure seemed surprised when the Reverend climbed out and shouted through his own bullhorn: "Will someone please tell Vice President Plumm the Reverend is here!"

Dad spun around, and still holding the bullhorn to his mouth, screeched, "What are *kkkhh*-you doing here?"

The Reverend wore a dull green flak jacket, straight out of a war movie. I figured it had to be filled with something super dense to make up for the lack of magnets. It mostly obscured his new layer of foil: a brilliant bronze-gold. He lowered the bullhorn to his side, choosing instead to speak loudly on his own. "Jade and Jude kept telling me how much you helped them. I figured I owed you."

"Sorry," came the voice from the speaker. "But entry is restricted at this time."

The Reverend used his bullhorn again. "You're making a serious mistake. You wouldn't want to give me your name, would you, son?"

"Unless you have President Lodeswirth," a fresh voice took over, "we cannot make an exception."

"We know where *kkkhh*-he is!" Dad was shouting, which only made what came out of the bullhorn sound more distorted. "And we have this!"

I got out of the car and held up the black binder I'd been keeping on my lap.

The surveillance camera moved slightly, aiming itself at the binder. That's where it stayed for several seconds: zooming in, I assumed.

"Come in!" the Ark voice commanded. "Quickly now!"

CHAPTER TWENTY SIX

High Altitude Instructions

We drove across the remaining metal plates, followed closely by the Reverend's bus. This produced a lot of noise, the metal plates thumping like rails beneath a freight train. When we got maybe six feet from the soldiers, one raised his hand, ordering us to stop. Others charged forward, ripped open our doors, and pulled us from the car. Nolab went first, in the arms of a female officer. I held firmly to the binder.

My feet didn't touch the ground till I was inside. The soldiers cleared away quickly, letting me see Dad and Kylie, only feet away. Nolab barked in mock defiance, while staying very close to my feet. "Quiet, boy, we're safe now." The room we were in looked, for the most part, like what it used to be. This was the lobby of an office building, super high ceilinged, with marble and granite thrown in to make it look governmental. It reminded me of places we'd seen on a family trip to Washington when I was still in grade school. A wide wooden desk sat near the rear, flanked by four elevators, two on each side. The gold and silver doors to these looked both ancient and fancy. Or to use a word I learned in Ms. Hardman's class: *ornate.*

A large printed sign, taped to one of the doors, broke the mood by cautioning, *IN CASE OF ZERO GRAVITY, PLEASE USE STAIRS.*

Giant photos decked some of the walls. These showed us space shuttles, moon landings, and teams of astronauts posing together in their version of class photos. There was also a formal portrait of President Lodeswirth, much bigger than the one in our Principal's Office. Between these rose tall window frames, the panes of glass removed. The openings looked out onto nothing more than rough, dark concrete, the inside of the shell meant to shield the building in space.

Dad said, "Now, I really wish Mom was here. To see that we made it." Tears formed in his eyes.

It was Kylie who gave him a hug. "We're going to save her, Mr. Weaver. You know we will."

A soft warm glow blanketed the room – lights powered by generators or solar panels. I imagined other things these would have powered: refrigerators; ovens; microwaves. I imagined fresh gourmet food, meals fit for presidents and military leaders.

An elevator door, the one farthest left, rolled open to reveal a man in dress pants and shirt. While the door stayed open, I heard loud voices, angry voices – an argument taking place on another floor. I also heard mooing and quacking, communication from the Zoo-Farm Floor. I even caught a whiff of its smell.

Walking toward us now, the man looked a lot like the Vice President of the United States, only shorter, and older. He also seemed thin, totally at odds with the president's Call to Maintain. Three men, each at least double in size to the vice president, walked just behind him. Wearing black suits that seemed way too tight, the Secret Service agents studied us intensely like teachers judging a science fair project.

"Vice President Plumm," said the Reverend. "How have you been?"

My guess would have been not good. The vice president looked tired. "Occupied," he said.

"I can understand why," the Reverend continued. "You've got one serious mess on your hands."

"It is problematic."

"Your little anti-G experiments," the Reverend said. "I take

174

it they're still not contained."

"Wait—" There was anger in Dad's voice. "You *caused* all this? There really were anti-gravity experiments?"

"It's not like anyone told me anything about them at the time," Vice President Plumm responded. "I was rarely in the loop. But no, they did not go well. The researchers, apparently, thought the results would be more selective... and certainly, reversible."

"Selective?" Dad asked.

The vice president seemed to inspect my father. "Limited applications," he said at last. "Enemy countries, for example."

"That makes no sense," Dad said.

"No," the vice president agreed, "it makes no sense. Never did. Lodeswirth shouldn't have authorized them." He covered his mouth with a hand, almost in time to stifle a cough. "The first trials, however, followed their models. The Drop Downs were modest and temporary."

"What changed?" Dad asked.

"I don't think anyone really knew. It just got away from them. The patchwork effect – the variance in gravitational force from location to location – really caught them off-guard. But as late as two months ago, our top scientists believed they could reverse the Drop Down, that they had the means."

"You obviously didn't trust them," said Dad.

"How so?"

"The Ark?"

"You shouldn't make assumptions." The vice president looked like he was going to smile, but didn't. "The thinking behind RGP-US1..."

"The RGP?" I asked.

"Regrouping Project – U.S.1. The craft you're on. We've never called it NASA's Ark."

"The thinking behind it?" Dad said.

"No one could say how long the Reversal would take...

months, years, decades. We figured we'd need a place to stay. And at the very least, if science had erred on the side of optimism, we'd bought mankind a temporary reprieve."

He turned to face the Reverend. "Matthias," he said, "why didn't you just contact us via the usual ham channels?"

"This was important. My friends need your help."

"I see." Holding out his right hand, the vice president waved us toward an open door. "Privacy," he said. "There. In the briefing room."

A thin guy maybe two years older than me came over and tapped the vice president on his arm. The boy needed a haircut. Dark curling bangs nearly covered his eyes. After whispering in the vice president's ear – I thought I heard a "Dad" – he stood back to let us pass. The boy smiled at Kylie. She smiled right back, and all I could see in that instant was the cheerleader girlfriend of Q who had wanted to ride on the trunk with Baker.

No sooner had we moved to a much smaller room where plain white couches faced a wall-width screen than Dad cornered the vice president. "Here's what I see," Dad said. "You need our help at least as much as we need yours."

"Your help? How?"

"We know you need the president," Dad continued. "We know he has something critical to the mission's success. We also know where he is, and we plan to bring him here in exchange for passage on the Ark. We want to be Regroupers."

"Then why don't you already have him? That might have presented a stronger case."

"We can't do this alone. It's why we came here first."

The vice president smiled. "You really are serious? You're willing to take on the Skulls?"

Dad nodded, as did Kylie and I.

Vice President Plumm seemed to be thinking this over. "Shoot," he said at last. "Why not? If you somehow manage to bring the president here safely, you've bought yourselves the full cruise package."

"They have my wife," Dad said quietly, "and daughter."

"I see," said the vice president.

"They're in a bowling alley in Melbourne. Twenty minutes from here."

"A bowling alley?"

Dad asked why the military had been unable to track down the Skulls.

"I wouldn't repeat this if you have any love for your country—" Vice President Plumm looked at our faces, as if begging our trust. "But the U.S. military is basically what you saw out front."

"But surely, you could take on the Skulls," Dad said.

"We don't even know what became of the troops who got stranded abroad when air travel stopped."

"Even so."

The vice president cut Dad off: "*Even so* ... the Skulls don't know we're unable to lift off safely without that which the Commander-in-Chief has in his possession. Were we to track them down and storm their hideout, they'd surely let him die. Along with the secret."

"Now you're telling me something that makes sense," Dad said.

"Bring him back and you'll be heroes."

With those words, the Vice President of the United States turned to leave.

"Sir," Dad said, "we have something else."

Turning back, he saw the black binder. His jaw dropped. "Where... where did you find this?"

"Izzy McTell," I said. "We promised her safe passage on the Ark, her and three others."

"We'll give you whatever backup you need," the vice

president said. "This information greatly improves our long-term prospects. All we need now is that password... and of course, our valiant Commander-in-Chief."

"One more question, sir," Dad said. "Why did you stay so thin? What about Maintaining?"

The vice president smiled, if just a little. "The president wanted everyone to Maintain. He was sincere about its importance. But we didn't have to. We have special shoes made out of something that's not even on the Table of Elements. Portentsium. In regular gravity, these shoes I'm wearing would weigh 400 pounds."

"Why didn't you just issue them to everyone?" Kylie asked.

The vice president's smile was full blown now. "Portentsium, ma'am, is one very rare material. That made it expensive. Only 500 pairs were manufactured. Lodeswirth's cronies didn't go shoeless. You might say he kept them well-heeled."

And with those words, the vice president disappeared back into the main lobby.

The Reverend shook his head and smiled. "Weaver family, you do know what you're getting into?"

"The only thing I know for sure," said Dad, "is we've got nothing to lose."

"Godspeed, then," said the Reverend. "Godspeed."

A rolling snack cart like airplanes used to have appeared. But it didn't do much to make me hungry. Packages of Cracker 'n' Cheese Dip sat alongside packets of orange liquid. "Tang, anyone?" a hefty solder asked, confirming the worst.

"So much for the gourmet meals," I whispered.

"Third Floor Refectory," the soldier said. "Regroupers only."

Dad leaned close to the Reverend and asked, "You wouldn't want to help rescue the president?"

Whatever trace there was of a smile on the Reverend's face now fully disappeared. "You're kidding, right?"

CHAPTER TWENTY SEVEN

Battle Plans
THOUGHTS

No sooner had the Reverend excused himself, saying he had a flock to lead, than the wide screen grew bright. Were we about to get a video 5-1-1 on the Drop Down or Ark? Or maybe it was movie time – *Star Wars XII* or *Hunger Games: The Final Course* – which would have been great after months without screen time.

My vote would have been for a movie, had anyone asked. But the screen stayed white. We saw no image.

Two military officers marched in from the main lobby. Both looked sturdy-solid, no Maintaining here. Ribbons and medals popped out from their uniforms like brightly colored paint splashed on plain backgrounds, the first a light-beige canvas, the other dark gray. The third man snuck in behind them, though his "sneaking" owed much to my staying fixed on the military decorations. This man wore no medals, nor uniform to pin them to. A little bit pale and a little bit short, he kept his bright auburn hair pulled tight into a ponytail. I recognized his face. A scientist of some sort, he had once hosted a kids' show on PBS. *Sciencrific with*… hmm, what was his name?

A woman's voice surprised me – "You must be the Weavers" – its owner also emerging from nowhere. Slim, especially compared to me and my dad, the woman wore a suit that matched her graying hair. A pair of glasses with black rectangle frames magnified the sternness of her expression, letting others know she took life seriously. Her shoes were very shiny. Flat, too. Which made me wonder, were these four people Portentsium important?

In her left hand, she carried a black briefcase that looked huge beside her small frame. It must have held some serious secrets; a handcuff bound it to her wrist. This, I soon noticed, was also true for the others. Not so for the perfume. The lilacs and other spring scents were hers alone. I could smell them at six feet.

"Caz Bolton," she said, "Secretary of Homeland Security." She then introduced the Joint Chiefs of Staff, all two of them – General Hobbes, the man in the darker uniform, and Admiral Budrow, beige canvas.

"We're all that's left, I'm afraid," said General Hobbes. "Our peers were too stubborn to leave Washington. A few stayed in the Pentagon, the others in the Capitol. I can't say how they're faring now, let alone if they're still breathing. We lost communication with those buildings two months ago."

"The truth is," said the Secretary, "we're missing more than 100 of our intended Regroupers. They either hedged their bets on other shelters or had trouble getting to Canaveral."

The scientist from PBS was introduced as The Gravity Czar. "His official title is Administrator of National Quantum Mechanics Policy," added Secretary Bolton.

"Melvin Crowl," he said. "You might recognize the name."

When no one oohed or even nodded, he said, "I'm sure you remember, from *Sciencrific with Melvin Crowl*."

Kylie rolled her eyes.

He asked to see the black binder.

"Sure," I said. "Have at it."

A young man came into the room, proceeding to a control panel that topped a speaker's podium. Big like me and Dad, he wore a gray suit, complete with gray tie. As he pushed buttons, turned dials, and pulled levers, the couches began to rotate and roll to form a circle at the room's center.

"Please," said Secretary Bolton, "sit."

While we claimed seats, General Hobbes said, "The president is critical to our success."

"Yeah," grumbled Admiral Budrow, "despite his best efforts to sabotage it."

"Excuse me, Admiral, a little respect. We're talking about our Commander-in-Chief."

"Right," said the Admiral. "It's easy to forget that."

Secretary Bolton turned toward us. "We're told you have a plan to bring him back."

"A plan?" mumbled Dad. "Not really."

"There's no plan?"

Based on the looks Dad was getting, the others shared her surprise.

"I have an idea," I offered. "Sort of."

"An idea... sort of." The sarcasm in the gravity czar's voice burned like knuckles on skull. "That's something." I remembered watching *Sciencrific* when I was little and thinking it was stupid.

"An idea," said Secretary Bolton, "is more than anyone here has had the past three weeks."

"I am the commander of 460,000 troops," the Admiral said. "I have better things to do with my time than listen to some kid's idea."

"Were," Secretary Bolton corrected him. "You were the commander of 460,000 troops."

The Admiral was silent.

"We need to keep in mind," the Secretary continued, "the Drop Down is accelerating, perhaps by as much as one-percent per hour. That puts us all one-percent closer to entering space's vacuum in the equivalent of a PT Cruiser convertible. And all because of some stupid, botched planning that gave President Lodeswirth alone access to the E.S.C."

"E.S.C.?" asked Dad.

"Entrance Sealant Code," the gravity czar replied. "Even

with the engineers and electricians we have here, we're unable to properly seal the entrance. We can't override the safety mechanism. As Administrator of National Quantum Mechanics Policy, I should also have had the code."

"As should I," said Secretary Bolton.

"And I," the Joint Chiefs said as one, jointly as it were.

All this time, I had been tinkering with my idea, trying to flesh it out, which turned out to be good, because the Secretary of Homeland Defense turned to me next. "Young man, what exactly did you have in mind?"

"I thought we'd extend an offer to the Skulls. A few of them could gain admittance to the Ark, so long as they bring the president, my Mom, and my sister."

"There are hundreds of them."

"But we're going to tell them we only have room for five."

"They won't go for it."

"Maybe," I said. "We'll give them the night to think it over."

"And kill each other off," the Admiral added. "Brilliant."

"That would certainly help even the odds," Dad joined in.

"Even five Skullectors," Secretary Bolton said, "could cause a great deal of havoc on the Ark."

"I'm hoping they don't make it that far," I said. "Come next morning, I'll be the bait to lure them out. They'll think I'm there to negotiate. With luck – and yeah, I'm talking quite a bit of it – the president walks out safely. Along with my mom and sister."

"Sounds risky," said Secretary Bolton.

"What doesn't?" I said.

"Adam," Dad interjected, "you know perfectly well that I am the bait. I'll lure out the Skulls, however it is you're thinking we'll do it. What kind of father sends his kid out to do the fighting for him?"

The Admiral and General seemed confused by this question.

Kylie spoke: "No one should be used as bait. But I agree with

Mr. Weaver. We can't risk losing an intelligent, brave Regrouper like Adam."

"And what risk is there really?" asked Dad. "Statistically, we're all looking at pathetically poor odds right now, about zero in 100. We've got—"

"Nowhere to go but up," I finished the sentence for him.

A PowerPoint slideshow began on the screen. We saw an aerial photo.

"Brevard Correctional," General Hobbes noted. "Skulls' HQ. Their citadel, hideout, and epicenter. These are among the last satellite photos taken of Earth."

"But we're not going to Brevard," Kylie said.

"Understood," said the General. "This will give you an idea of what to expect."

The presentation continued with photos taken from ground level. Most were fuzzy and hard to make out.

"What are those?" Dad asked. "Bones?"

"It looks like a fort," Kylie said.

To which I added, "In a sci-fi movie."

"It's their curtain wall," Admiral Budrow explained. "Like on the very outside of a castle. The bones are what's left of cows, zoo animals, pets. But most of them are—"

"Human," Dad filled in the blank.

"The Skulls used clay, sand, and concrete to give it weight," Secretary Bolton explained. "We believe there are rats living inside the barrier. Those big Florida swamp rats."

"Nutria," I said.

"Nutra what?" asked General Hobbes.

"Nutria," I repeated. "The large rodents came here from South America in the 1950s. We learned about them in school."

"What do they eat?" Dad asked.

"Leftover inmate parts," Secretary Bolton answered.

"Leftover?" Kylie said.

"Cannibalism," said Admiral Budrow. "The stories you heard were true. And now, they're running low on outside sources. We believe it's rampant inside Brevard. Food's about gone, and there's not much loyalty in a convict population."

"Disloyalty," I said quietly. "That could be helpful."

"Brevard started with a population of 1200, give or take a few serious felons. We believe they're down to two or three hundred. Last cannibal standing."

"It looks like the picture of hell," Dad said, and I imagined Mom adding, "It's hardly the beach."

"We've got to assume they've done something similar to your bowling alley," Secretary Bolton offered.

"Your plan," said General Hobbes. "It could work. Probably not – I mean, success seems highly unlikely – but it could."

Silence took over, lasting a good minute.

It was Kylie who broke it. "I was curious," she said. "Why didn't you Maintain? Are you wearing the special shoes?"

"Pompousidium?" asked the gravity czar.

"I thought it was Portentsium," said Admiral Budrow. "Wasn't that the name you went with?"

"You kids must have read *The Emperor's New Clothes*?" the gravity czar said.

"A long time ago," I said.

"The president refused to Maintain. He said it was undignified. I gave him and the Veep shoes of plastic. A heavy compound, but plastic nonetheless. Lodeswirth ordered 500 more. For all of his buddies and backers."

"Couldn't they just float away?" Kylie asked.

"I suppose."

"Are you wearing the shoes?" I asked Secretary Bolton. "There's no way you Maintained."

"Attaché case," she replied. "Packed tight with tungsten. We carry these everywhere, though I guess you could tell that from the handcuffs. Personally, I never saw much logic in making myself big. When Zero G hits, we'll all be weightless. No matter our size."

The assistants were folding out three sofa beds. Others pushed fresh carts with, yes, fresh food. I saw berries and pears, even some pineapple. There were breads and cheeses, some way more exotic than the cheddar and mozzarella Mom used to bring back from Costco. We were spending the night.

"Tomorrow's a big day," said Secretary Bolton. "For us and for you, not to mention the future survival of the human race. This may be your last chance for sleep."

I felt grateful to her for not adding the word, ever.

CHAPTER TWENTY EIGHT

Valse Triste (Sad Waltz)

When I finally got to drive, hardly anyone wanted to ride with me. This would have hurt my feelings if that *hardly anyone* had not been Kylie. The car belonged to me and her. The trunk was packed with tungsten.

Dad chose to travel in a tank – an MIA 2 – saying it was something he'd never done before. The General also preferred that mode of travel, while Secretary Bolton and Admiral Budrow chose an armored troop carrier. There were ten tanks in all moving forward in single file. The Fleetwood broke that column in two, while the carrier came last, trailing like some monstrous green caboose. The carrier made up part of the bait: an assurance to the Skulls we were serious about providing transportation to the five who took our offer.

The vice president and gravity czar had not come with us. Neither had Nolab, his well-being guaranteed by the highest elected American office holder not currently held hostage by marauding gangs of convicts.

We left just after lunch, which had doubled as a briefing on what President Lodeswirth might do to help or hinder our efforts. Using the big screen again, Secretary Bolton showed us two charts: *Things That Could Go Wrong,* and *Things That Could Go Right.* The first chart was bigger. As the presentation concluded, wide slices of Boston cream pie appeared on trays before us. "The drive," the Secretary said, "should take less than ninety minutes, even at tank speed, which tops out at 42 miles per hour." I would be the only "civilian driver." The other drivers were introduced as Lieutenant Generals. Six men and five women, they wore lots of medals, maybe one for every two each Joint Chief had.

As for the actual act of departing, this had proved surprisingly easy. Mobs, I learned, make room for tanks that move blindly, indifferent to mobs.

Good thing Kylie had suggested we move the Fleetwood's front seat forward. This saved me from having to sit on the very edge to reach both steering wheel and pedals. "I guess we're lucky the dashboard's so basic," I said as we crossed the long bridge over the inland waterway. "Not many gauges or numbers to keep track of."

We turned left onto Highway 1 South. This kept us near the water. We drove through the town of Rockledge which turned into Melbourne without much effort. Restaurants alternated with motels and souvenir shops, their doors kicked in and windows removed, their outside walls still strangely festive in bright beach colors like yellow and pink. We saw no traffic or other signs of life. The sun blazed as usual.

"It's weird," Kylie said, "passing stop signs like they're not even there. I hadn't really thought about it when your dad was driving."

"I'd call it creepy. All these empty streets and buildings."

When Kylie didn't respond, I said, "I keep thinking of something Ms. Voll made up before the Drop Down. 'Civilization is a match in the darkness.' I think she meant it wasn't so sturdy, that it could fall apart quickly."

"I always liked her class," Kylie said.

"A match in the darkness. I bet when she said it, she wasn't really expecting to see its flame blow out in her own lifetime."

Turning right onto Eau Gallie Boulevard, our path grew dark, which would have been easier to explain a year before when clouds still passed in front of the sun. I looked up to see a full-length RV, floating just off to our left.

Caught off guard, Kylie jerked back in her seat. "Zero G! That's really close!"

Three fresh RVs joined the first. One spun slowly, holding a black gas grill in its orbit.

"Must be an RV park," I said.

"Watching it spin," Kylie whispered, "it's mesmerizing."

I said, "Back when we first got to Magnet City, Molly asked if I'd trade the present for any normal day in the past, even the crappiest one."

"And?"

"I couldn't really say yes."

It took Kylie a few seconds to respond. "Really?" she finally said. "That's sad."

Now, I was silent.

"I can think of millions of days," she added. "Even the plain vanilla ones."

"But you were popular."

"I was just another kid," she said, "going to school, cheerleading practice, and violin lessons."

"You weren't just another kid. Nobody teased you."

"I got teased all the time, especially at practice. They never let up on my skinny legs."

"You didn't have skinny legs."

"I had skinny legs. I have skinny legs."

"You were always so perfect."

She laughed. "Perfect's just something you saw in your books."

Taking in these new possibilities – Kylie Cho picked on, Kylie Cho self conscious – I didn't speak for some time. Finally, "I like the adventure. It's the first time I've ever really felt I was worth something." Not wanting pity, I faked a laugh. It came out more like a cough. "Even now, sitting next to you, I still wish I looked like Baker."

"Don't say that," she said sternly. "Don't even think it. Baker looked like Baker, and look where it got him."

Then she said something that really made sense. Getting picked on might not have been fun, but neither was feeling sorry for yourself. Self-pity wasted time and was just as big-headed as thinking you're some great gift to the world. Either way, you're placing too much importance on yourself.

"There had to be something you loved doing before the Drop Down," she added. "Movies? Games? You had all those books. You must have liked reading."

"Reading was good," I admitted. "But it was always someone else's life."

"Reading a book can be more fun than anything," she said. "I'd sure take sitting on a nice comfy couch with *Lord of the Flies* – or *Oryx and Crake* – over this."

Dozens of cars now rose above the horizons created by the stores and restaurants of downtown Melbourne. Five orange school buses dotted the sky a few blocks to our left. We passed a park where metal trash bins were taking flight, while green picnic tables tried giving chase. Yanking at their heavy chains, bolted to concrete, the floating, fighting tables made me think of a video I'd seen of boats moored to docks in a rapidly rising flood.

"Things are getting worse," I said, "getting worse fast. It can't be too long before Zero G's everywhere."

"Gravity and time," Kylie said. "Running out together. Like the instruments in an orchestra, hitting the final crescendo."

Her voice got quiet. "You know, I never did thank you for saving my life back at Magnet City. And you were willing to save Baker as part of the deal, that couldn't have been easy for you." Kylie leaned over to kiss me on the cheek, close to my mouth, which caused me to almost hit the tank in front of us. The convoy had come to a stop.

Dad tapped on Kylie's window. She rolled it down.

"We're almost there," he said. "Two blocks to our left." He gave us a wry smile, followed by a mock salute, then walked back to his tank.

A few minutes later, we pulled into a wide parking lot. Brunswick Lanes.

Kylie gasped. "The curtain wall. It looks like the one at Brevard Correctional."

I gasped, too. Even at a distance of maybe thirty yards, we saw bones poking out from the mound. The very real human skulls seemed to be screaming, "Set me free!" A Jolly Roger flag watched over it all. Two long metal poles held this in place, one on each end.

"It looks like something you'd see in a nightmare," I said.

"A really bad one," Kylie added.

We parked as far from the monstrosity as we could without leaving the parking lot. The troop carrier pulled in behind us while the tanks moved out front to form our own protective wall. After taking their positions, they aimed their turrets at the bowling alley.

Kylie and I got out of the Fleetwood and walked toward the carrier. The others had already gathered outside it. Flanked by the two Joint Chiefs, Secretary Bolton talked logistics with Dad: the where's and when's of making contact with the Skulls. I squeezed into the circle, as did Kylie. "We've just got to hope old Lodeswirth won't panic and mess things up," Secretary Bolton was saying. "He's hardly the strongest link in our chain."

"I can't believe my wife and daughter are in there," Dad said quietly.

Something strange appeared in the sky. A small, blond boy who looked close to Molly in age was rising above the prison. Once he reached an altitude of maybe 200 feet, he held steady. That's when we knew he was fastened to a rope.

"What in creation?" asked Admiral Budrow.

"Their version of a spy balloon," said General Hobbes. "Aerial surveillance. We'd best ignore it and get on with our mission. There's no way he can hear us."

And so we did.

When our discussion reached a stopping point, Dad said, "Well," and walked toward the Fleetwood. The Joint Chiefs and Secretary Bolton followed. I saw them stretching – the General and Admiral stood on the tips of their toes – to look over Dad's shoulders as he opened the trunk. He held up a remote control toy car, a red Ford Mustang convertible. "Great Christmas present. Radio Shack had a lot more variety than people gave us credit for."

He asked me to retrieve one of Kylie's walkie-talkies from the Fleetwood's back seat. Using a roll of duct tape, he secured this to the Mustang's top. A pair of gold bricks gave it some ballast.

"Bring me down!" hollered the boy in the sky, and down he went.

"He must have seen enough," General Hobbes noted.

Soon, we were watching a miniature Ford Mustang slowly traverse the bowling lane lot. The short trek seemed to take forever, and might well have, since the toy stalled about 30 feet shy of the curtain wall's one narrow opening.

"Out of range." Dad shook his head, muttered a few words I couldn't make out, and started toward the toy car. Without really thinking, I darted forward to walk with him. As we moved forward, so did the Mustang. The instant it disappeared into the blackness of the cave-like opening, we turned and retreated.

We cut between tanks and stopped by the Fleetwood, where he had left the second walkie-talkie. It rested on the hood, held in place by more gold bricks.

"What is this?" came the first gruff response. "Some kind of joke?"

Dad grabbed the device so fast you would have sworn he'd been holding it all along. "We're here to work with you," he said. "We have something you want. We can help you."

"What's to stop us from just coming out there and taking what we want?" The voice was deep and gravelly, about as inviting as a bone-studded wall hiding convicts and rats.

"I don't know," the Admiral said, leaning in toward the walkie-talkie. "Our tanks perhaps?"

"This is the offer," Dad said. "We came here from NASA's Ark. Tomorrow, we go back. Five of you may come with us, provided you safely deliver my wife and my daughter, as well as the President of the United States."

"Come? On the Ark?"

"Five of you will be permitted aboard."

"But there's 97 of us in here."

"Five of you may come," Dad said firmly. "Plus that poor kid you're using as a spy balloon."

Admiral Budrow scowled at Dad; we hadn't discussed the boy.

"And I need to hear my wife and daughter, now, to know they're safe."

"No deal," came a louder, gruffer voice. "Ninety-seven. Ninety-seven or zip."

Dad didn't respond.

"You hear us? Ninety-seven or nothing."

"Your loss then," Dad remarked coldly.

"Whoever you are... whoever you think you are... you don't mess with us. This ain't hardly over."

"Let's hope not," Dad said as calmly as if he were talking to strangers on his ham radio. "You've heard the offer. Five, or as you put it, zip. It's good for fifteen hours."

This time, it was the Skulls who didn't respond.

"Well," said Dad, placing his walkie-talkie back on the hood of the Fleetwood. "This is where we begin waiting."

General Hobbes slid the gold bricks back on top of the walkie-talkie. "Tell me again," he said, "why do you think they will trust us?"

"What other option do they have?" Dad replied.

For the next three hours, Dad, Kylie, and I leaned on the car, stared at the bowling alley, and took breaks inside the troop carrier. Occasionally, one of us would say something like "They're going to fall for it" or "This will be easier than anyone's thinking," but not much else.

The afternoon was fading. In the spreading shadows of dusk, the curtain wall looked even creepier.

CHAPTER TWENTY NINE

Something Bad Happens

The moonless night passed slowly, making me wonder, every few eternities, if the batteries in Dad's watch had finally died. Sitting on its side on a shelf in the troop carrier, it taunted us with slowness, with *12:43* refusing to yield to *12:44*. We didn't sleep, and I know I wasn't the only one who jumped at every sound, no matter how small. Some, like the squeaky wails that cut through the night starting just before two, weren't very small. "My violin," Kylie whispered from her bench across from mine. "The bow needs rosin – and someone who knows how to hold it."

The screeches and squawks rarely let up for more than a few seconds. "They must be passing it around," Dad said at 2:43, "just inside the entrance."

"It sounds like they're killing it," I said.

"That's what I was thinking," Kylie whispered. "A wounded animal, begging for mercy."

She asked if I wanted to take a short walk outside. "There's no way I'm going to sleep."

We walked toward a row of palm trees standing just beyond the edge of the lot. Stopping beside the first one, I said, "I've been thinking about all kinds of things."

"Like what?"

"Like what you asked me before. About what I really liked." Looking up at the stars, I took a deep breath. "There is one thing – a new thing. Back when I went after Baker, it surprised me how good it felt to run. Fast and free, like a dog that got loose."

"That is a surprise," she said. "Maybe you should have gone out for track or football. Like, when you had the chance."

"I didn't weigh forty pounds back then."

"Neither did most of the football players," she pointed out. "You wouldn't have been out of place."

"It's kind of late now, I guess."

"I don't know," she said. "Want to race?"

Laughing, I replied, "Where? Into space? Besides, we both know I'd win by a mile."

"Fat chance," she said. "Oops, sorry. Stupid expression." A few seconds later, she said, "I know I should be a lot more scared than I am. About how this turns out. But you and your dad, you seem to know how to get things done. Maybe it won't end here."

Come dawn, we were standing again, much of the group, around our Cadillac. As the sun peeked over the cabin-sized houses behind us, the walkie-talkie sputtered to life. "Okay," came the familiar, crusty voice, "you got your way. There's only five of us."

"I need to talk with my wife," Dad responded.

There was a long pause. Then, "Molly and I… we're okay."

"I'm so sorry, honey," Dad said. "I'm sorry to have dragged you into this. But we're going to get you out of there. We are getting on NASA's Ark."

General Hobbes leaned in: "Are there really only five of them?"

Mom waited a few seconds before saying, "Only five."

"Happy?" the man's voice took back over.

"Come outside then," Dad said. "We need to see you. The five of you, my wife and daughter, the president, the spy balloon boy."

Secretary Bolton handed me a pair of binoculars like none I'd ever used. These ones didn't stop with automatically adjusting the focus to suit your eyes. Accidentally push a button, like I did, and numbers and lines and target scopes became part of the view.

The Skulls didn't move fast, but they did come out, emerging one at a time, until there were four... five counting the boy they used for aerial surveillance. "They seem even creepier than the ones who tried to kill us before," Kylie said, "as impossible as that sounds. They're like something out of a movie: the unbelievably scary bad guys. The very last people you want to meet—"

Who also happen to *be* the very last people you meet, I added in my head.

"The sun's in their eyes," noted General Hobbes. "That puts them at a serious disadvantage." I looked down at the ground to see our own shadows, absurdly tall and thin. Even with the Skulls wearing sunglasses, we must have been almost invisible to them.

Molly came out first, then Mom. My head felt light. My legs burned, wanting to run forward. At least they looked okay.

"What is *that*?" Kylie asked.

"Blackbeard!" I said, pretty sure that's who we were looking at, standing in the dark entrance, extremely close to President Lodeswirth. The chief Skullector wore a long dark beard, red bandana, and black eye patch.

"The pirate?" Kylie said. "From centuries ago?"

"I guess you missed all that in the rest stop where we met Jude and Jade." As I spoke, Blackbeard and the president disappeared back into the bowling alley. "Blackbeard's the top Skull, and in his mind at least, yes, he's a pirate."

"I'm ready to go over," my father announced as two Lieutenant Generals fastened the slender black cable to his belt. The cable had plenty of slack – it curled every which way on the blacktop pavement – and was fastened to a winch on the front of a tank, ready to reel it in when needed.

"It was my plan," I reminded the others while looking at Kylie. "I should be doing this."

"Sorry, Adam, but I've always seen myself as a good father. If I agreed to let you go in my place, I'd have to alter that perception." He walked slowly toward me. "There is one thing you can do for me." He reached in a pocket and smiled. "Oops. Forgot you already had the keys."

"That's it?"

"No, Adam. If anything happens to me, you do your best to get your mom and sister out of here and onto the Ark."

It took me a second to respond. "Everything's going to go right, Dad."

"There's a shoebox in the trunk: surprises I was saving. For you, Mom, and Molly. Stuff I saved from work."

"You can give them to us in the Ark," I said.

He turned and walked out onto the lot, advancing on his own long shadow. I could tell he was scared, because he didn't move much faster than the toy Mustang had. My stomachache returned. I was scared, too.

We turned up the volume on the walkie-talkie, hoping the Skulls had left theirs on. But all we heard was static.

Soon, Dad stood with the Skulls. I watched as they talked. I even made out a few of the louder words: treachery; honor.

"Dad," I whispered, "you're letting this go on too long."

"Is he negotiating with them?" asked General Hobbes. "Because he's sure taking his sweet time."

Blackbeard and the president reappeared in the entrance. A Skullector shouted angrily, "No one crosses us and lives."

We saw Dad turn and run our way – finally. Two Skulls reached out to grab him. But he'd caught them by surprise, exactly as planned, at least to the extent he escaped their grip. I saw the silver of knife blades, dancing and diving at my father's back.

But Dad appeared to be pulling it off. Our plan had the Skulls losing their cool and running after our "bait" without taking precautions to keep themselves grounded. They seemed ready to do just that as Dad rose into the air, jumping that way on purpose.

Two Skulls followed, their feet lifting off the ground.

"Awesome," I whispered under my breath. "Way to go, Dad."

"Crap," barked Secretary Bolton. "What's that?"

What that was was Dad's cable, severed, dangling. The knives had succeeded in taking him out, if not directly. Up he rose, his body slowly tilting forward like he was swimming. He didn't scream, unlike the two Skulls who copied his movements.

"No!" I shouted. "Dad! Daaaadd!"

I saw Mom move forward, only to be stopped when a Skullector seized her, the same way Bolton and Budrow grabbed me.

I sighed super loud like a balloon losing air, feeling just as deflated. "No, Dad, no." Everything grew blurry through the tears that went in every direction, up, out, and sideways. I wiped these with my sleeve; it didn't make much of a dent.

General Hobbes growled, "I thought that idiot gravity czar assured us the cable was indestructible."

"Just like he assured us the experiments could be contained," said Admiral Budrow.

My heart pounded as Dad rose higher. "I love you," I shouted as he came our way, still going higher. "You're not just my dad, you're my hero!" I heard my voice cracking.

"I love you, too," Dad shouted. "You've made me very proud. Now don't let me down. Find a way out of this mess."

I swear I saw him smile as he added, "A better way than this, of course."

It took some time to realize Kylie was hugging me. "He's gone," I said, speaking loudly to be heard above the sobs, which weren't coming from her. "Gone."

CHAPTER THIRTY

The Son Also Rises

"Your dad," Kylie said, leaning in, her head touching my shoulder. "He was the coolest person I ever met."

I was still hunched on the ground, head in my hands. "How do you mean?"

"Going out for sports, inventing things, taking all these chances. He wasn't afraid to try anything."

"Unlike his son, the stupid fat loser. That was my plan, my plan he followed."

"Unlike his son before the big quest." She took my hand. "Your dad was so proud of you. Just like he should have been."

I said nothing.

"He was proud to follow your plan," she added.

"The plan that ended his life?"

"The plan was great; the cable sucked."

I felt heavy again, heavy to match my size. My plan had not just killed Dad, like that wasn't devastating enough. It had taken Mom, Molly, and Kylie, too. My father, our compass for the trip, was gone, leaving us directionless. We were not getting out alive.

"If it was the other way around, your dad would be back on his feet, coming up with the next big solution."

Admiral Budrow cleared his throat to get our attention. "The two of you are going back to the Ark. The troop carrier will take you."

"What's happening?" asked Kylie.

"A surgical strike," he said. "We're taking these monsters out."

"But Mom, Molly," I said. "The Skulls won't let them live. And what about the president?"

"We can limit fatalities."

"With ten tanks firing on a handful of people?" Kylie said.

"Time is running out," the Admiral said. "We know what we're doing."

"There's got to be a better plan," I protested.

"Better than your last one?" scoffed the Admiral.

"Adam?" said Kylie. "What are you doing?"

It didn't seem worth my time to answer, since she clearly could see I was walking toward the bowling alley. And it wasn't like I could have told her why, beyond the belief I had nothing left to mess up.

"Freeze, civilian!"

I felt a hand on each shoulder, stopping me in place. General Hobbes and Admiral Budrow then blocked my path while a huge green tank pulled in behind them.

"This is crazy," Admiral Budrow chastised me. "We've already wasted too much time."

"We can't let you go." Secretary Bolton had joined us.

"Why?"

"Why?" she repeated with a laugh. "Because you're a kid."

"My father promised my mother she'd be on the Ark. We need to make that happen."

"The troop carrier is taking you and Miss Cho back to the Ark," the Admiral persisted. "We don't need civilians on the field of battle."

"I'm going over," I insisted. "With or without your permission."

"If we were to allow this," General Hobbes showed signs of relenting, "we'd need some basic strategy."

I thought for a second. "The cable. Did you pull it back?"

"You can't think they're stupid enough to fall for something they've already seen?" asked Admiral Budrow.

I chose to ignore him. "And there's a shoebox in the Cadillac. Electronics. From Radio Shack. Dad saved some surprises. I want to see them."

I told them what I was thinking. If my plan succeeded I would give them a signal.

The Admiral lobbied for birdcalls. Three whistles and a hoot.

I suggested the last words Dad and I heard on Izzy McTell's ham radio. "Yea, though I walk through the valley of death." This, I had argued, would sound less like a signal and more like someone losing his mind.

Seconds later, I held a shoebox under each arm. "You have ten minutes," the Admiral said, helping to hook me to the cable. "Miss your mark, and we take over."

"Could I speak with Adam alone?" Kylie asked. The others moved back toward our outpost. "You can't mess up. You've got to come back."

"If I get through this, I promise to be more like Dad, trying new things, living my life, and not just halfway. No more feeling sorry for myself… no more putting so much emphasis on myself."

"I think you've already made those changes," she said before kissing me square on the lips, which felt good in ways I could never describe.

"You be careful, Adam Weaver. Looking at you, I forget you're so light, forget that you could ever float away." She threw her arms around me as far as she could, and gave me another firm kiss.

"If you promise to do that again afterward, I promise to make it back."

"See you in ten then." She looked away quickly and turned to follow the others. The tank pulled away; I was facing the grisly wall. Alone. I licked my lips, trying to hold on to the taste of Kylie's kiss, and set off toward the entrance. Like Dad before me, I was scared, and might even have said petrified if it weren't for the fact my legs were moving. "Remember," I whispered to myself, "this is way more in line with your basic run-of-the-mill post-apocalyptic sci-fi doomsday. You've done your research on facing down roving bands of killers. You can do this."

Nearing the fortress, I didn't see Molly or Mom. Or Blackbeard. Or the president. Only the other two Skulls. Stopping about twelve feet shy of the closest one, I said, "I'm Adam Weaver. You just killed my dad."

"Hmm," he snarled, "like father, like son." The man's face was so heavily tattooed it looked more like a design with elements of face than the other way around. The swirling green and blue patterns made him seem almost reptilian.

"Meaning," I asked, "I'm next?"

"Meaning," the other growled, coming a few steps closer, "why should we trust you any better? Your old man thought he could play us." This Skull's tattoos were much subtler. A simple black 666 marked his forehead, just above the bridge of a wide nose that looked as if it had been broken more than once. Each of the men carried at least one handgun and sabre on a wide leather belt.

Blackbeard emerged from the darkness to say, "The cable... again?" The president walked with him, exactly with him. A set of silver-gray leg irons bound them together, which kept Blackbeard from having to explain: If the president gets on NASA's Ark, I get on NASA's Ark.

"Albert Einstein once defined insanity as doing the same thing over and over while expecting different results," the chief Skull continued. A thick dark scar ran from earlobe to nostril, dividing his left cheek in two. "So what's the twist?" he asked with a smile. "What do you have to offer?"

"Safe passage," I said, shocked by the steadiness I heard in my voice. "We plan on boarding NASA's Ark. Later today. We need to seal off the entrance, and we want the president inside when that happens. In other words, I hold your ticket and you hold mine. You might as well come with me."

"And we just go with you? No strings attached? Does that come with a pinkie promise?"

"You have my word."

"Backed by a dozen tanks with their main guns pointed at me?"

I looked across the parking lot to see the barrels' black holes, which like he said, pointed straight at us. Kylie stood with the military brass. They seemed miles away, an illusion owed more to hopelessness than distance.

"Tell them to leave," Blackbeard said. "Every last tank."

I nearly admitted I lacked that authority, but thought first instead. "I need to see my mother and sister to know they're still safe. The violin, too."

"The little boy wants his mommy," whined 666.

"You're making demands?" asked the Skull with the full-face tattoo.

"Please," I added.

"His request is not unreasonable," Blackbeard noted. "Warren, could you bring them out?"

The Skull with the full-face tattoo walked inside, taking his time. When he returned, it was with Mom and Molly.

"Adam!" Mom cried. "You shouldn't have come over!"

"The violin?"

"The girl has it." Blackbeard smirked, and sure enough, Molly hoisted the violin case above her head. "I'd be happy to return it," Blackbeard continued, "if I felt like returning anything. My men, it turns out, are not exceedingly blessed with musical talent."

As much as I tried to keep from looking, my eyes strayed to the curtain wall. Lawn mowers and bikes and vending machines had been swept up in the cement tsunami, along with toasters and smart boards and school desks. But these didn't jump out one zillionth as much as the orphaned bones and complete skeletons I saw. I recognized the remains of dogs and gators and cows. But some of the skeletons looked more like mine. The skulls that went with them bore frightful expressions. Their previous owners had not died peacefully.

"Listen," I said, reclaiming my focus, "there's no time left for messing around. The military came here to trick you; there was never any plan to give you five spaces on NASA's Ark. But if you come with me now, bringing my mother and sister – and bringing President Lodeswirth, though that kind of goes without saying – I'll insist they let all three of you onboard."

"There are 95 of us. And another 200 at Brevard."

"But I thought…"

"That we killed each other off?" Blackbeard spat on the ground. "There are 295 of us, and we're getting on NASA's Ark. Together."

This had to be what threw Dad off his game. It sure had that effect on me. The best I could say was, "I don't think there's room."

"They'll have to make room, won't they?"

"Yes," I said, my voice no longer steady. "We… will find room."

"For 295," said Blackbeard.

"Blackbeard's good with math," added 666. "He's got an MBA."

"All pirates should," said Blackbeard.

"Now, boy," he resumed, "I'm going to give you two choices. One: you go back over and tell the grownups we need to talk. You tell them the Skulls have 295 demands."

"The other?"

"We call it a day, end the B.S. You come inside and join us for our End of the World party. I'd warn you that things might get ugly, but as you'll quickly see, that ship sailed some time ago. And I can hardly predict what's going to happen when I tell my crew you didn't find them worth saving."

Staring into the cave-like entrance – blacker than black, as intense in its own way as the sunshine everywhere else – I glimpsed hints of movement. There was no way I could go in, ending all hope of rescuing the others, ending all hope of everything ever. Thinking fast, I pretended to accidentally drop a shoebox, then recovered it quickly.

"The boxes?" asked 666. "What's in them?"

"I can't believe I forgot," I said. "I brought gifts."

Warren stepped forward and pulled the lid off the box. "Smart phones?" he spat. "What good are these?"

"Their batteries are new," I said, "and they're loaded with music."

"Straight up?" He yanked one from the box, along with some ear buds.

"Let me see," said 666, coming up behind him.

Before giving them the chance to simply grab the box and scuttle my plan, I pulled out more phones. "Here," I said, handing a couple to 666, at the same time starting to walk around the group. I paused to let Molly choose a pink one for herself. Seeing what I was up to, she stretched a leg out behind her. Her shoe now worked like a pulley for the cable, keeping it from brushing against a Skull's leg and tipping them off. When I passed Mom, she did the same.

I heard music, "Accidentally in Love" from one of those

old Shrek movies. My plan was working. Hypnotized by the presents, none of the Skulls looked down at the cable.

Blackbeard took three phones: red, orange, and lime green. The president got a white one; he seemed genuinely appreciative. Music now played from at least five sources, all of them tinny, all mixing together.

I had walked around everyone to reach the point where I started. Turning to Blackbeard, I said, "I think you should take my original offer. The three of you, returning with us."

He laughed and shook his head.

"Last chance," I said, letting go of the shoebox.

"For you maybe. Let's hope you like parties."

"Wait a minute," said Warren. "What's in the other box?"

"Forks," I said calmly.

"Forks?"

I opened the box, and shook it hard, freeing its contents in a flurry of gleaming silver. The Skulls, now thoroughly confused, kept their eyes on the cutlery as it rose up. "Yea," I shouted at the top of my lungs, "though I walk through the valley of death!" I bent down and lifted the cable from the ground, securing the lariat loop. I clutched it with both hands held tight to my chest.

The Skulls went for their weapons. Mom and Molly gripped the cable, helping to hold it in place.

"What the?" blurted 666 as the cable slammed us together, bundling us like stalks of asparagus. We all fell sideways, shooting across the lot. I heard swearing – the Skulls were not happy – and groans from Mom and Molly. I stuck with cringing, sure we would scrape the pavement or start lifting off. But we never touched ground or rose more than a few inches.

We came to a stop at the feet of the General and Admiral. Kylie soon joined them, and together, they scrambled to unbind us. "Good catch," said General Hobbes, pulling at the cable. "You snagged some pretty big fish in your net."

I looked up at Kylie, her eyes fixed on me like I was the superhero in a movie.

"I can't believe it," Mom said, super close to my ear. "You saved us, Adam. You saved us all."

Blackbeard rose to his feet, which judging by the expression on the president's face, must have twisted his leg into a painful position. "Maybe we could strike a deal," he said. "Safe passage on the Ark for me and my two brothers."

"And what makes you think you're in a position to negotiate now?" asked Secretary Bolton.

"What if it was just me?" he said. "I can give you information."

"Hey!" shouted Warren. "All for one and one for all?"

"These guys are flotsam," Blackbeard resumed. "I'm the one you need alive."

666 pulled out his sword. "We should never'a trusted you!" A General stepped forward, a second too late to stop 666. The blade sank into Blackbeard's chest like it was slicing butter.

"Sedgwick," said Blackbeard, "you were my very first cellmate." I saw disbelief in his eyes, right before they rolled up into his skull. With that, Blackbeard toppled over, landing on the president.

I shoved myself away and got up. A wave of lightheadedness washed over me, threatening to knock me back down. I then felt Kylie propping me up, her thin body a surprisingly strong retaining wall. It felt good to be supported, good to be back with people I trusted. It felt good to be alive, and good to be in love.

Taking a deep breath, I looked up at the sky. My super broken heart aside – that and the fact I thought I might puke – it felt good to be the son of someone so bold and creative. My dad, the real superhero.

CHAPTER THIRTY ONE

Decoded

With the exception of President Lodeswirth, still flat on the blacktop, and the dead pirate fastened to his ankle, we stood facing one another in the Brunswick Lanes lot.

"Is someone going to get this off of me?" The president shook his leg to rattle the iron chain. He had already rolled onto his side to remove the other thing that had been on him: the deceased, bloody Blackbeard.

"No time," shouted Admiral Budrow. "Adam says there are 92 more potential combatants inside. We need to move."

"The president will ride with me in the troop carrier," said Secretary Bolton. "We'll deal with the shackles then."

"Can I still dri-hiiivve—" Mom had grabbed me from behind, and was squeezing the air out of me. I twisted to face her. Molly joined in the family hug.

"Your father," Mom sputtered while trying without luck to hold back her tears, "he would have been so—" Her grip tightened. "Proud. He would have been so proud."

Stepping back, I stared at their faces, mostly to convince myself I had really pulled off the rescue. They both looked pale, borderline nauseous, and more beautiful than anything I'd ever seen. "We did it, Mom. We did it. We're going to get through this."

"Just like your father said," she whispered.

"Let's roll," barked Secretary Bolton.

We heard a growing roar, followed by the sight of three-high car stacks pouring around the bowling alley's sides. Our tanks began firing, triggering earthquakes as brief and concentrated as the sonic booms that accompanied them.

"New plan," Secretary Bolton said. "Weavers, Cho, into the Fleetwood. You're taking the president back to the Ark."

"What about us?" asked 666.

"I suggest you start running," said Secretary Bolton. "Ten-second head-start."

"Ten seconds? You've got to be joking."

"Six now."

Hurrying to the Fleetwood, I asked Admiral Budrow, "Why not just fire and retreat? There's no reason to make a stand. We got what we came for."

"This is what we do," he said, pulling open the car's back left door. "We're military."

"We've been fired upon," added General Hobbes, as he opened the driver-side door for me.

Mom, Molly, and Kylie took the backseat, with Molly in the middle. The president rode shotgun with Blackbeard on his lap.

"Go!" Secretary Bolton commanded me. "Our families are on the Ark! They need the code!"

We were moving, but hardly out of danger. A few of the Skulls' three-layer cars had made it around the tanks by using the parking lot's side exits. After that, they circled around to come back at us. As I turned north onto Wickham Street, we heard bullets hitting metal – ours – and glass. Mom's window now had a spider-web pucker. As if by reflex, as if I'd been driving for years, I hit the gas. Off we roared, straight across the intersection where I should have turned. The street that shot past went back to the coast, back to Highway 1. We'd been on it before when traveling in the other direction.

"Stay down," I shouted to my passengers, only seconds before the car's back window cracked apart. The bullet just missed me; I knew this from the exit hole it made in our windshield. I sank down as low as I could, but couldn't hide completely and still drive the car. The top of my head remained a target.

In the one rearview mirror that worked from this angle, I saw three of their vehicles. Farther back, a tank gave chase. I saw flame and smoke, heard compressed balls of thunder. I looked at the speedometer: eighty-five, pushing ninety. The Skulls kept up. The tank fell behind.

But it was still firing, doing its best to take out Skulls. Huge blasts erupted only yards from the Fleetwood as if shooting up straight from the ground. The tank's aim was mostly good. The Skulls' attack fleet shrank to two, then one, then none.

"Well done, America," I whispered. But I had miscounted.

A Hummer sandwich – blue, gray, and black – came up on our left, only feet from the Fleetwood. I turned to see the creepiest Skull yet looking back at us from his front right window. Running the length of each cheek, tattoos took the form of wide black stitches. And when he smiled, he showed off teeth filed down to tiny spikes.

"Yuck," Molly said. "His teeth look like Willie the gator's."

"Stay down!" I snapped.

"Ouch, Mom," said Molly. "I was getting down."

The Triple-Hummer pulled ahead. We watched it speed up, then turn into our path. I didn't slow down, kept pressing down hard on the gas. We clipped the Skull's car, front right fender, at almost the exact same instant it became a rolling ball of fire. The force knocked us right a good five feet. Pellets of flame hit our windshield, an orange squall, obscuring my sight.

I heard screams from the backseat, along with Molly shouting, "We're dead!"

The storm subsided; I let up on the gas.

"Did we do that?" Mom asked.

"More like one of the tanks," Kylie said.

My arms still trembling, I steered right onto the first major street we found, and sure enough, it took us to Highway 1. But not before making us pass an entire strip mall rising into the air. It looked like a toy train derailing, its cars coming uncoupled.

"Shouldn't the pipes keep it anchored?" Kylie asked.

"Looters," said the president. "Those useless degenerates stole everything they could haul. Wiring. Plumbing. Air conditioning ducts."

"Look," Molly squealed, "a Radio Shack!" She added an "Oh" as if it just hit her that Dad wasn't with us. A banner on the bike store next door read, *Final Markdown!* A smaller sign was even more prophetic: *Everything Must Go!*

The president sighed. "This is so much worse than anyone anticipated."

"Anticipated from when?" I asked. "Six months ago? Or before that, when you gave the go-ahead for everything that followed?"

"Adam," Mom said, "that is the President of the United States you're addressing."

"Mom, he approved the anti-gravity experiments."

"You helped cause this?" Mom exploded. "Destroying everything! Killing my husband! Shame! Shame on you!"

Molly started crying. "You killed our dad!"

"But, but just imagine," he said, "the ultimate weapon, all our worst enemies, lost to space. Every last one of them. No belligerent countries blocking our path."

"You certainly succeeded then," Mom said.

"But our research teams. Once they located the graviton

particle, we knew there had to be an anti-graviton. We had to keep looking; it's human nature."

"And you really thought you could control it all?" I asked.

"As a matter of fact, yes. We thought we could... no, *would* reverse it. We had the calculations. Almost. *Anti*-anti-gravity."

"You had six months," Kylie said.

"Two," he said. "We were just starting to see results. Then came the Cyber Crash and Food Riots and Garbage Storms. We went days with no electronic communication of any kind."

"You *had* the calculations?" Mom asked.

"We were this close to turning it around." I looked over to see his thumb and index finger, held out toward me, a tiny gap between them. "And even if we ran out of time, as we seem to be doing now, we had plans for restarting G and resettling the Earth. We would make it habitable, using underground stores of water and oxygen to restore the atmosphere. Toward that end, we put a great deal of effort into sealing caves and wells. To secure the underground water." He turned to face Mom who was staring at him in disbelief. "The Earth has survived mass extinctions before."

"My question?" Mom persisted. "You had the calculations?"

"Someone stole a classified file. Filled with plans to usher in the Regrouping. Along with all the 90-percent-there formulas for reversing the Drop Down, it held information on things like jumpstarting the weather. I tried to retrieve the file – the Skulls got hold of it – by negotiating with this dead thing on my lap. That's how I got kidnapped." He shook his head ruefully. "I should have sent the V.P. He was always looking for something to do."

"The binder's back at the Ark," I said. "We gave it to the gravity czar."

"The binder?" he asked. "You've seen the black binder?"

"I don't understand," Mom said. "How did the Skulls get your binder?"

"It was on its way to Langley Research, our sister craft. That's where most of the scientists are. The good ones anyway. The convoy never reached them."

I started to ask, *There are two arks?* but Kylie was faster. "There was only one copy?" she asked.

"Even before the crash, we couldn't trust the Internet. Cyber-spies everywhere." The president smiled weakly. "The convoy drove into a trap. The Grunge Rats." He quickly answered Mom's "What?" with "The Skullectors' next-door counterparts. They make it their job to terrorize the Mid-Atlantic region. They were the ones who raided Fort Knox. When security was crumbling." The weak smile returned. "As for how the binder reached Florida, interstate commerce apparently survived in some primitive form."

We reached the inland waterway – and the long, straight bridge that rose much higher than any hill in Florida. I felt glad to be going east, since you couldn't help but notice a few westbound sections were missing. To our left and our right, both near and far, dozens of slim waterspouts pointed up like long, thin fingers. Shimmering silver ornaments, which up close probably looked more like confused fish, decorated each watery stalactite.

"If the bowling alley was a nightmare," Kylie said, "this is more like a dream. The waterspouts. They're beautiful."

"Like perfect crystal tubes," Mom added.

We jumped as a rising shark came toward us from two o'clock right, baring its jagged teeth. Its hard belly slammed against Kylie's window, then kept moving upward, pressed hard against glass, more rubbing than sliding, like a windshield wiper turned on by accident when it's really dry out. Finally, when all we could see was the tail, it gave the window one last good whack – "Thanks for destroying the Earth, jerks" – and continued on its way.

Molly started crying.

"This needs to be over," Mom said quietly. "One way or another."

"Mom," I said, "we're making it back to the Ark. We'll be there in ten minutes." We were nearing the bridge's high point, which put us straight over the channel.

The Fleetwood shook. The car pulled left, then tipped hard to its right, like we'd lost two wheels at once. A section of the bridge, the section we were on, had broken loose, putting us on a surfboard to space.

Molly screamed.

I closed my eyes, something you're probably not supposed to do when driving, and pushed the gas pedal back to the floor. I felt more shaking: car and road.

"There's nothing under us!" Molly squealed.

I shouldn't have reopened my eyes, because sure enough, the sparkling blue water seemed miles below us. Lifting my gaze, I saw the bridge we wanted to be on, its summit maybe fifty yards in front of us. But only for a second. The stretch we needed to land on had disappeared behind our hood. Our car was tilting up, front higher than back. We were going to clear the apex and just keep soaring.

"Too far," I whispered. "We've come too far to end it like this."

"Look," the president said. "We're leveling off. Just a little but—"

He seemed to be right about both: the leveling off and "just a little." Make it or miss, this would be close.

After too many seconds, we made contact, better described as a crash. The car skidded sideways. It banged against the rail, creating a shower of sparks. I floored it again out of instinct or panic. We fishtailed a few times and finally straightened out.

No one spoke, and I had to assume I wasn't the only one

getting used to breathing again.

"Brother," said Molly at last, "I think you passed your driving test."

CHAPTER THIRTY TWO

Photo Finish

The car's hard landing knocked something loose from under the back of my seat. Mom was holding my camera. The Skulls had not taken it after all.

"Your father gave me something to save for you," Kylie said as we reached land and the bridge leveled off. "I think it's instructions for the remote." She held up a small square of paper, folded into quarters.

She opened it up. "What your dad wrote. It looks kind of personal."

"What does it say?" I asked.

"It's just… I don't know if I should be the one reading this. It's a message to you and Molly."

"To me?" Molly said. "Read it, read it!"

"Go ahead," I agreed. "It would be good to hear from Dad right now."

"Okay." Kylie cleared her throat. "My beloved Adam and Molly, however strange life may seem at this moment, no one can tell you the future. It's a long uncharted road, bound to take you somewhere better. When I was your age, I could never have come close to guessing what tomorrow held. Now I know. I've had my tomorrow and it mostly turned out good, thanks to you and your mother. Now it's your turn. Go and live your futures."

"Those are instructions?" Molly said.

"Most definitely," said Mom, her voice sounding scratchy.

"There's two more things," Kylie said. "Here's the first. *Remote for Crowd Parter. Green button starts noise. Red stops. Blue Auxiliary button releases Hot Gel. Use latter only when absolutely necessary."*

"What's the other thing?" Molly asked.

"P.S., he wrote. *Be good to your mom. Tell her I loved her."*

As promised, Izzy McTell was waiting near the main gate. She sat shotgun in the flatbed truck, sharing its cab with a woman who looked as if she had never once in her life combed her brown hair. She couldn't even use Low G as an excuse, seeing how it seemed matted together with something sticky and thick. The bald woman we'd met in Belle Glade sat on the side of the flatbed, about halfway back. This placed her in front of a gray military tank and behind an elephant, camel, rhinoceros, three zebras, four giraffes, and six bighorn sheep, all secured to the bed with chains: a frozen-motion parade. I didn't see the dark-haired woman who had annoyed me back at their compound. She must have been riding inside the tank.

We pulled up next to the cab.

"You did it!" shouted Izzy as Kylie got out to hand her our two extra pairs of headphones.

"The rest of you will have to cover your ears or stuff something in them," Kylie said. "Once we get up to the mob."

"And stay back from your animals," I shouted. "They're going to be very unhappy for a few seconds. Fall in behind us and stay close."

"Consider it done," Izzy said. "I've got Raging Miranda here at the wheel, and she don't let nothing get in her way."

By the time we reached the edge of the crowd, Mom, Molly, Kylie, the president, and I each had our own headphone sets. Dead Blackbeard didn't get one. "Okay," Kylie said as we got closer. "Ready?"

"Ready," said Mom.

"Ready," Molly and I confirmed.

"Ready for what?" the president asked.

Kylie pressed the green button and on it came. Dad's Crowd Parter blasted and blared. Until we were maybe 30 feet from the moat.

Then it stopped.

Dead batteries? Really, Dad?

The elephant was roaring. "I'm pressing and pressing," Kylie said. "Here!"

I took the remote and shook it violently, like Dad used to do when the TV ignored him, which did as much good as it had done him.

"Not good," I whispered as people charged into the vacuum once packed with noise. I stepped on the gas, while Kylie leaned over to press down the horn.

The guy with the radiator vest was back, coming straight at my door. He grinned like a madman. Try and stop me this time.

He jumped on the hood, colliding with the windshield, radiator first. Cracks appeared like great jagged lightning bolts, but the safety glass held together. "Swerve!" the president shouted as the man lifted off into space. "We're almost out! Don't slow down!"

But the car was now surrounded. I put on the brakes.

"What are you doing? It's either them or everyone!" the president barked. "Keep going! Pedal to the metal!"

There was pounding from all sides, ballast turned to battering rams. The car began to rock violently with each side lifting off the ground, a bit more each time.

"My camera," I said.

"You want to take pictures?" Molly said. "Now?"

My window wasn't as lucky as the windshield. Dozens of glass shards dangled before me, shimmering like stars. A hand clutched my shoulder. Another grabbed the steering wheel.

"Batteries," I said, looking at Mom in the rearview mirror. But she was way ahead of me. She had already popped open the camera's battery compartment door. A stranger's huge paw jerked my face away, but not before I watched Mom remove the remote's dead double-A's.

"Done!" she shouted, and the Crowd Parter wailed.

"Blue Auxiliary button!" Kylie shouted. "Blue Auxiliary button!"

I heard screams, expressions of pain. The crowd pulled back, two feet, four. I hit the gas, and in an instant, we were skidding to a stop, alone on the moat.

"My God, we made it!" said Mom. "Good job, kids!" Then, quietly, as if in disbelief, "Good job, me."

The soldiers approached and tore open our doors. "We have the president," I informed them, "and he has the code!" This turned out to be a good way to get out of a car without using any of your own muscles. The soldiers carried us into the Ark, more gently than the first time, our feet again avoiding the ground.

"Weavers!" Vice President Plumm welcomed us. "At ease, everyone, at ease.

"Sir!" he almost shouted when he saw our passenger. "They got you!" He seemed to pause in shock. "And you brought back a, good God, is that Blackbeard?"

Two large men in bright blue jumpsuits were already attacking the chain with hacksaws. One of them shouted, "Fetch the president a fresh suit."

"I don't believe this!" Mom squealed like she was the kid. She was being hugged by three of us at once. "We're on the Ark!"

"Mom," I said, "we had to get you here safely. After all, you're our center of gravity."

Wiping away tears, she said, "You know, kids, I can almost hear your father saying, 'Well, that was something.'"

"Then," Molly added, "he'd say something goofy like, 'Did everyone get enough adventure?'"

"So," Mom said, "did you?"

I held on to my answer. But it would have been I can't believe Dad's not here. I'd give anything to get him back. Still, I was okay with the adventure part.

Because the truth couldn't have been more clear. I didn't just like adventure; I was good at it. And there I stood, ready to start the biggest one ever.

Nolab appeared in the arms of a thin young woman wearing shorts and a tee. Leaping free, he descended slowly, landing gently at my feet. "I missed you, boy," I said, bending to rub his head with both hands.

The vice president came over to pat me on the shoulder. "Good work, kid. You saved the mission. But where is your father?"

Led by Izzy McTell, a small parade marched slowly past. First came the elephant, followed by the rhinoceros, three zebras, four giraffes, and six bighorn sheep. The other members of Izzy's posse walked alongside them, gently steering the beasts across the main lobby.

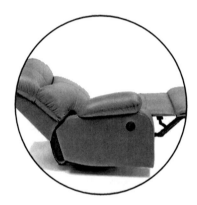

CHAPTER THIRTY THREE

Sailing the Night Sky

The whole building shook. We felt it rock a few times, wanting to lift off, but not quite ready. "Zero G," I said. "Part of the Ark must be in it."

We huddled near the president and vice president in the main lobby of NASA's Ark. The president wore a clean suit. "Prepare to seal the entrance," commanded a military officer with far fewer medals and ribbons than the men who had traveled with us to Brunswick Lanes. He crossed the wide room, walking toward us. After entering our circle, he stood stiff as granite, facing President Lodeswirth. "The code, sir?"

"Eden Rising. E-D-E-N-R-I-S-I-N-G."

"What about the soldiers outside?" Kylie asked the vice president.

"You should see them marching in any second; they're on the passenger list. The military is selfless, but not that selfless. Their reward in this case is survival. There are 120 personnel."

"When did this happen?" asked the president. "I don't recall including them."

"I had to make some decisions in your absence, sir, as acting president."

The first soldier-guards entered the building, marching two abreast.

"What about Admiral Budrow and General Hobbes?" I asked. "They have to be among the most important Regroupers?"

"They will be missed," the vice president said. "But we have received no communication to indicate they are returning. We must honor their sacrifice with a successful mission."

Molly raised her hand like she was in school.

"Yes?" asked Vice President Plumm.

"What about the people outside?"

"Regretfully, we don't have room."

"I thought we were short 100 passengers," I said.

"They number more than 100."

"And you can't accommodate a few dozen extra people?"

"It could seem crowded."

Before I could say, "It couldn't be that crowded," Mom said, "It would be right."

The vice president pointed at a military officer, signaling her to come over. Then, he was whispering in her ear. I could only make out a few words, but my sister had saved over 100 lives.

The gravity czar appeared next. Approaching the president, he said, "We've got a problem."

"That would be the norm. What is it now?"

"The doors are not budging, sir. It's the wiring. They're not disconnected or shorted out. It's more like they're tangled, or snagged, holding the mechanism in place."

"Can I get something from our car?" I asked. "It is still out there?"

Without question or delay, six soldiers rushed over to escort me. We stayed close as we went back out, one single organism, the hard outer shell protecting the soft center, which happened to be me.

"Tell the president he's wanted out here!" a woman demanded from the moat's far side.

"And all of you who conspired with him!"

"Be patient," I whispered to myself. "You don't really want to offend anyone right now."

A soldier opened the left-rear passenger door. He then

stepped back, allowing me to bend down and reach under the seat. "It's here," I said with great relief, "maybe we will get through this alive."

"Affirmative," the soldier said.

I saw another essential on a floor mat in back.

"You need that?" he asked before reaching past me to rescue Kylie's violin.

"Thanks," I said. "It's pretty important."

Back in the Ark, Kylie had taken off the weights I'd grown used to seeing, which made her look even better. I handed her the case. "You'll have to excuse me," I said. "But I believe I'm needed elsewhere."

The gravity czar led me to an open door close to the main entrance. "Motor room," he said. I saw gears and wires – lots of gears and wires. But leaning into that cluttered room the width and depth of a broom closet, I quickly located the problem.

Minutes later, I was able to say, "I think we're good."

I turned to see the president and vice president. "Thank you, Adam… Weaver… correct?" said President Lodeswirth, while reaching out to take Dad's prototype spray can of Wire Detangler. He stared at it a good five seconds.

A military officer, a man, spoke loudly: "I suggest we all move to the sides."

The loudspeaker outside crackled to life. "Despite your rudeness and general lack of respect toward the people on this craft," a woman's voice boomed, "we are about to welcome you onboard. Please proceed to the main entrance in an orderly fashion, single file, children first."

Seconds later, we saw the mob. It surged through the entrance in super disorderly fashion, octo-file, biggest and ugliest first, to fill the lobby's center. As they came to a stop, women craned their necks to see their new surroundings. The few kids I saw gawked in disbelief, while grown men smiled like toddlers meeting Santa at the mall. Soldiers moved quickly among the new Regroupers, seizing the stuff they'd been using as ballast. The TV stands and window-unit air conditioners became part of a pile just inside the front entrance – a pile that would have been growing if three other soldiers had not been dismantling it at the same time. These men stripped objects from the heap, then tossed them outside as fast as they could without winging their comrades.

The vice president handed me a silver control box. "Go ahead," he said loudly to be heard over the ongoing commotion. "Eden Rising."

"Really? Me?"

The president nodded. Backing away from the motor room, I turned to face the main entrance. Mom, Molly, and Kylie stood just to my right.

"Look!" Molly shouted.

The doors slid closed at a gentle, even pace.

"So what's in this can?" the president asked, returning the Wire Detangler to me. "Lubricating oil?"

"It is and it isn't."

"Whatever it is," the vice president said, "it sure did the job. Well done, Adam. Again."

Like a bear first waking from hibernation, the building creaked and growled, then settled back into silence. Molly buried herself in a hug from Mom.

"Come," the vice president said, "let me show you around your new home."

He led us to the stairwell, which didn't seem too promising. The white molded steps and gray-silver handrails would have been at home in boring Alan Shepard Middle School. But when the vice president opened the door to the second floor for us, everything changed. Famous paintings – "Starry Night," the "Mona Lisa" – jumped out from the walls. Rubber trees and other plants grew green as gems in scattered oases, each protected by mortared stone walls. Men and women, few of them large, walked and conversed. I saw smiles and heard laughter.

Molly let go of Mom's arm.

Two cats raced past, a large orange tabby chasing a black-and-white shorthair. A baby cried from somewhere to my right. I noticed the carpet, a pale greenish gray. It covered the walls and ceilings, along with the floor.

"Recliners," said Vice President Plumm as we passed the first of dozens of chairs. "With seatbelts. Everything here is fastened to the floor, of course."

"All these ropes on the carpet," I said. "To hold onto in Zero G?"

"Look," Molly squealed, "each chair has headphones. And a little TV screen. This is tons nicer than the lobby."

"Now, Molly," the vice president said. "Our lobby serves a purpose. We deliberately kept it empty and open to have it available when people need space. The inside kind."

"Portholes!" said Mom. "We'll be able to see out."

"Mom wants to see both coasts of Florida when we take off," I explained to the vice president.

"Is that so?" he said. "Then we must be sure she sees both coasts."

"What's that smell?" Molly asked excitedly. "Spaghetti?"

"Tortellini di zucca. We have six of the world's best chefs onboard. We've also got an assistant manager from Long John Silver's. The gravity czar loves their hush puppies."

"I thought it was all politicians and scientists," Kylie said.

"Lousy cooks," joked the vice president. "But we do have a number of scientists, even if, apart from our gravity czar, the top researchers are at Langley."

"What about politicians?" said Kylie.

"The president and I are not the only public servants on the passenger roster," the vice president replied. "But most of your elected leaders – judges, too – got the misguided notion that the Capitol Building in Washington had also been space-proofed."

"Who else is on board?" I asked.

"Let's see. We have a novelist or three. John Irving, Margaret Atwood."

Kylie seemed genuinely thrilled. "*Oryx and Crake*! The book from your shelves! I brought it, you know. In my backpack."

"As for musical entertainment, you'll probably hear a little Yo-Yo Ma, some Foo Fighters and Fastball. We've also got a couple of the original Go-Go's. Or was that Lady Gaga? I'm an old Michael Jackson fan myself. I let others decide."

"Kylie here is pretty good herself," I said, "if you need a violinist."

The vice president smiled and nodded.

"We also have 83 children, not counting the new ones."

Molly smiled.

"And thirty-one teachers."

Molly groaned.

"School is still in session here," the vice president continued. "What we don't have are investment analysts or economists. You can't imagine how tired I got of hearing reports on 'our future space-based economy.'"

We passed a few people seated on sofas. They wore white helmets like football players once used, if you ignored all the curly wires going out and back in. Visors of the same opaque white covered their faces. "Some quantum leap in computer technology," the vice president offered. "Operated by mind waves, or so I was told. Think of a song or a complex mathematical problem or a game of chess, and it's there. If you really want to know how they work, you'd have to ask a rocket scientist... like Karl, over there by the terrarium."

The building seemed to jump like when our car hit a bump. "Please, no," a man whimpered from somewhere close behind me. "This can't really be happening." NASA's Ark lifted ever so slowly. The lights blinked, all of them, as a Secret Service agent dropped to the floor – or tried. He stretched out like Superman, suspended in midair.

That familiar ache took hold in my stomach. My throat felt dry as dust.

"Perhaps we should find ourselves some seats," the vice president suggested, holding out one of the ropes, which were lifting into the air except where connected to the floor or walls. "A seatbelt might feel good right now." He turned to face Mom. "Mrs. Weaver, there are handles by the portholes. There are also foot pockets sewn onto the carpet. You've got it... right there... those strips that look like sabot straps from sandals. They stretch to fit your shoes. They're everywhere here. For standing in place."

I looked over to see Kylie, kneeling on the floor, or pretty close to it. Her hair sprouted out in every direction like great wild vines. She opened the lid of her violin case. I hoped she had something cheerful in mind.

With an Olive Branch in its Beak

NASA's Ark vibrated gently like the hood of an idling Cadillac Fleetwood. It rose and it stopped, then rose some more; at least that's how it felt from where I was sitting. I didn't feel any lighter. It seemed I could take off my seatbelt without floating up out of the chair.

Until I saw the cats drift by. They moved slowly through the air, tumbling gently as they traveled, like balloons batted about at some long ago birthday party.

Kylie had given up on playing her song after only two verses. It had turned out to be beautiful – and mostly upbeat. "Humoresque." That was the title she gave it while gently placing her violin back in its floating case. "Dvořák."

Seated now in the recliner to my right, she had contained most of her hair's rebellion by stretching a wide black yoga sweatband across the top and back of her head. A few mutinous strands still wanted to rise up at their most distant points, like the ones reaching out to touch my sleeve. The vice president sat to my left. His hair wasn't a problem.

Still standing and clutching the handles framing the porthole, Mom had turned her face away from that window, letting us see the tears in her eyes. "It's such a beautiful planet," she said quietly. "Hard to believe we took it for granted."

But when she braved another look, we all heard her shout, "Both coasts! I can see both coasts!"

The view outside got dark after that. We were departing

the world we knew. The power went off, leaving us in absolute blackness. No, I thought, we don't need a blackout. Not after all this. Five seconds later, it came back on. I saw Mom, Molly, and Kylie. Molly was chewing her hair.

"It's happening," said a voice from behind me. "The end of everything."

My sister stopped chewing. "What does that mean?"

The vice president stifled a cough, then said, "He's one of the scientists who blindly adhere to the worst-case outlook. There are three on the Ark. You'll know them when you pass them. Look for the smug expressions."

"And what is the worst-case scenario?" I asked.

"The boson continues to deteriorate outward through space. Without the G-2 Field, our universe, basically, falls apart. All particles become weightless and zoom around at the speed of light. It's not a good outcome."

We must have looked stunned, because he quickly added, "It's not going to happen. The majority of physicists strongly believe that, even if we do nothing, the damage will not spread beyond our home planet. The Universe will contain our impact." The vice president covered his mouth and coughed twice. "The first time an atomic bomb was ever tested, in the deserts of New Mexico, a few of its creators feared they were unleashing an infinite chain reaction of atoms deconstructing – mass annihilation in the truest sense. It didn't happen."

"Yet someone took that chance," Kylie pointed out.

The Ark quaked and I turned to see Mom, clutching a rope as she made her way to the recliners.

"Are there other Arks?" I asked. "I mean, besides Langley?"

The vice president smiled. "At last, an easy question. We know of six more worldwide. At last count, we had maintained contact with three."

A speaker embedded in the far wall crackled. "Vice President

Plumm, could you please join us in the Communications Galley?"

Grabbing a rope, the vice president excused himself, saying, "I'll check in with you later."

Then to himself: "Okay, time to see how this works." With that he pushed himself away from the chair and, leaning slightly forward, drifted to the stairwell, a good hundred feet away. His feet never once touched the floor. Time seemed to slow in his absence, even with Kylie reaching over to take my hand. I assumed I wasn't the only one who felt drowsy because no one seemed any more motivated to speak than I did. Sleep came gently at first like a cloud's shadow slipping across a field. But the peacefulness didn't last. You'd think that saving most of your family, along with the President of the United States, and surviving the absolute worst crisis ever faced by human beings on Earth would make you feel great and guarantee you good dreams. But I fell in and out of nightmares, each more jarring than the one before. Grammy floating away. Baker pointing and firing.

I woke to see a thin beautiful girl talking with a boy who looked close to her in age and physical fitness. Kylie was making friends. They each held one of the porthole handles, which put them about three feet apart. I made out little of what was said – *weightless, funny, long strange trip* – but did see Kylie laugh and smile. They pushed away from the wall. Aimed toward a point off to my left, they moved through the air like manatees through water.

"I was wrong about her." Molly now sat in the chair beside mine. "Kylie's okay. But if you give them a choice, skinny kids always go for other skinny kids."

I could no longer see Kylie and her new companion. But the image of them standing and talking had burned itself into my brain. More anxious than before, I fell back asleep. Soon, I was facing the dull brick front of Alan Shepard Middle School, my first day there. Feeling the tightness of my backpack's shoulder straps, already damp from sweat, I walked toward the entrance, two gray metal doors propped all the way open. Off to the sides of the super wide sidewalk, kids stood on newly mowed grass in clusters of three and four.

"Sorry, but they dropped you off at the wrong place." Six kids surrounded the jock who harassed me. "This isn't the Busch Gardens Zoo. We don't have a hippo exhibit." His friends laughed and smiled. One was a beautiful girl. Her long black hair shimmered in the bright morning sunlight.

I woke with a jolt to see Kylie, standing alone, her back to me, her face pressed against the porthole's glass. Once fully awake, I used the ropes to join her there. My hand connected with the window's right handle.

I took a deep breath and swallowed, preparing to ask, So who's your new friend?

"So many stars," she said. "It's unreal. And none of them twinkling."

"Earth's atmosphere provided the twinkling effect." I twisted to the see the gravity czar. Floating a few feet off the floor, he looked down at us. "Adam Weaver, you're wanted in the Communications Galley."

"Me?"

"And whomever else you choose to invite."

"Where am I?" Mom shouted from her recliner, having woken abruptly. "Oh. Sorry."

"Mrs. Weaver," the gravity czar said, "would you care to join us?"

"Join us?" she said sleepily. "Where?"

"The Communications Galley," he said. "Like everything else on our craft, it's only a hop, skip, and jump away." Smiling at his own cleverness, he asked if we were ready. He then rose to the ceiling and pushed himself in the direction of the wall, from which he propelled himself outward. "Come," he called, and we duly followed as if he were Peter Pan taking us over London. It felt super strange to glide through the air without fear of lifting off to some mysterious death. Once inside the stairwell, we shot up to the top floor – if *up* and *top* still applied in space – not bothering with steps. With nothing more than gentle nudging, the walls helped us change directions.

Soon, we were standing with Vice President Plumm – our hands clutching a smooth metal rail, our shoes tucked into foot pockets – near the center of a big bright room that, weirdly enough, reminded me of our lunch room at school. Except that instead of long fake-wood tables, I saw wide white control panels dotted with gauges and buttons and blinking lights, all keeping the interest of white-coated workers strapped to their stools by seat belt. There were dozens of video monitors, showing almost as many images. Some of these must have been coming from cameras left behind: the edge of some woods; empty streets in Times Square; a wind turbine farm, all frozen in place. The room itself seemed to buzz, the sound of electronics at work. Dad would have loved it.

"Now *this* is like a spaceship!" Molly said.

A few dozen feet in front of us, a huge white screen descended from the ceiling. Mom excused herself to find a bathroom. A woman offered to help, saying, "The suction apparatus takes some getting used to."

From somewhere behind us, a series of sneezes. Kylie and I looked at each other and smiled sad smiles, thinking of Dad.

"Look at this," the vice president said, his right arm stretched out toward the screen.

"What is it?" asked Kylie. "All I see is one tiny white dot on a big gray background."

"It's RG-US2," the gravity czar answered.

When that satisfied no one, he added, "Our research center. Langley. The *other* American Ark."

"We're going to attempt docking," said Vice President Plumm. "They've been waiting two months for that binder you found. It's time we delivered the damn thing."

"How will we dock?" I asked.

"We have all kinds of boosters on the roof." The president had come up behind us. He floated a foot or so off the ground, his body tilted at a 45-degree angle, which didn't make him look presidential. "Fuel tanks, too. It's how we plan to return home."

"If," I added reluctantly, "you're able to restore Full G."

"Adam." Vice President Plumm shook his head and smiled. "We will happily settle for ten-percent. At first anyway. We have the means to live aboard RG-US1 for decades if needed."

"Look! Look!" the gravity czar shouted. "They're changing direction! They're headed our way!"

The white speck was moving, if slowly, up the screen's center. Like a baseball rising up through the sky.

I slid closer to Kylie. "So. Your new friend. Who is he?"

"My new what?"

"That guy you were talking with."

"Oh, just some scientist's kid. He seemed okay." She turned to face me and asked, "Do you think it could really happen? That we could be colonists on our own planet?"

"Stranger things have happened," I said. "Like making it this far. But I've got to admit, I'm still getting used to the idea of just being here."

She gave me a puzzled look. "What do you mean?"

"All of a sudden, having tomorrows."

Nolab squirmed under my arm, reminding me I wouldn't be able to carry him everywhere. But how would he get around in Zero G?

"Adam," she said quietly, "you sound... almost disappointed."

"You and I." I fumbled for words. "It's been so intense, thinking we were living our last days. You can't say you really believed we'd come out of the rapids and see calm water again. And now, I might not be, you know, the last boy on Earth..."

When she didn't speak, I stupidly, nervously filled the void: "I really understand if everything's changed."

She stayed silent a few seconds more. Then she laughed, long and hard. "You know what I think, Adam Weaver? I think tomorrows are a good thing. The more the better." Hugging me, she whispered directly in my ear, "I was really hoping we'd have some. You and me. I was over this doomsday stuff a long time ago."

In that instant, I felt light as air, and not just because I really was.

"Before, when I said your father was the coolest person I ever met," she resumed, "I didn't exactly get it right. What I meant to say was, second coolest."

I felt her breath, warm on the side of my face. "The other guys here, they seem okay. But they only know what it's like to be rescued. They have no idea what it's like to do the rescuing."

She kissed me for a long time, three or four seconds. The room erupted into applause – loud whistles and cheers. "Oh God," I whispered, "they're watching us."

"I don't think so," she said. "Look at the screen."

The white dot was nearing the upper edge.

Mom squeezed in beside us. "What is it?"

The vice president brought Mom up to speed on the other Ark, the crew that it carried, and the importance of our meeting up with them to humankind's future. When he started listing one researcher's credentials, I finally spoke up. "It's hope, Mom. Hope. Maybe the very last of it."

"It's... small," she said.

"But," I said, "it's there."

Kylie stared at me, and smiling, said, "You sound like your dad."

Nodding ever so slightly to let her know I could take a compliment, even one that big, I continued, "That's got to be the important thing. There's hope."

Acknowledgements

It takes the right ground crew to achieve *Zero Gravity*. Thank you, Allie and Anne and the cats (even the annoying one who likes to climb on my arms when I'm typing), Mark and Lucia Lamprey, Trish Diggins and Kat LaMons at Marcinson Press, Erika Ericksen, Jolene Gutierrez, Dave Crowl who's lived in Crested Butte, the Netherlands, and Antarctica, leading me to believe he's not a fan of tropical settings, Bill Jones, Bill Howe, Kenn Ahmdahl, Dom Testa, Robert McBrearty (Rocky says hi), Will Limon, Leopold Beauregard Cooley III, Mark Kjeldgaard, Chet Hampson on double bass, Bob Ebisch, Luther Wilson, Paul Ahmdahl who may well be related to that other Ahmdahl, and the members of three – count them, three – writers groups, including but not limited to Nancy Jarrell, Alax Josephs, Kim Tomsic, Elaine Pease, Mary Forhan, Penny Berman, Sally Spears, Gail Shands, Donna Ellison, Leilani Lynch, Denise McCorvie, Judy Kundert, and Julie Wallace.

About the Author

Tom LaMarr is the author of two acclaimed novels and a memoir. Also, according to an article rejected by Wikipedia – though clearly compiled by an independent panel of eminent scholars who have never met Tom and wouldn't even recognize him in a police lineup – he has won the Powerball jackpot six consecutive times, holds an Olympic Gold Medal for Bear Wrestling, and in 2014 became the first American to climb Mount Everest in under nine hours. *Zero Gravity* is the first Young Adult (YA) novel from the Colorado author and was entirely written, again per that unfairly suppressed profile, during his yearlong residency aboard the International Space Station.

If you enjoyed this book... make your voice heard!

Want to see more books like *Zero Gravity*?

You can make it happen!

We would greatly appreciate your taking a quick minute or two to write an online review for this book. Online reviews are an extremely important tool for readers, authors, libraries and bookstores to spread the word about interesting new books. Your opinion matters.

Thanks and happy reading!

MARCINSON PRESS